"Molly, why don't you give Mr. Richardson a break?"

Lark looked down at her pink-cheeked child before glancing at the pink-cheeked professor.

Still giggling, Molly asked, "Why?"

"Because maybe he wants a rest—that's why."

The child looked up at Cole. "Do you want to rest?"

"I ain't dead yet, pardner. Let's ride," he shouted, scooping her onto his broad back and galloping out of the kitchen.

It was wonderful to have a man around the house, Lark thought. Especially a man like Cole. Knowing it was only for a few days made it easier to reconcile her growing attraction to him. Soon he would be back on his side of the wall, and she would stay on hers, and life as they knew it would go on.

Too bad, though...

Dear Reader,

Ah, summertime…those lazy afternoons and sultry nights. The perfect time to find romance with a mysterious stranger in a far-off land, or right in your own backyard—with an irresistible Silhouette Romance hero. Like Nathan Murphy, this month's FABULOUS FATHER. Nathan had no interest in becoming a family man, but when Faith Reynolds's son, Cory, showed him *The Daddy List,* Nathan couldn't help losing his heart to the boy, and his pretty mom.

The thrills continue as two strong-willed men show their women how to trust in love. Elizabeth August spins a stirring tale for ALWAYS A BRIDESMAID! in *The Bridal Shower.* When Mike Flint heard that Emma Wynn was about to marry another man, he was determined to know if her love for him was truly gone, or burning deep within. In Laura Anthony's *Raleigh and the Rancher* for WRANGLERS AND LACE, ranch hand Raleigh Travers tries her best to resist ranch owner Daniel McClintock. Can Daniel's love help Raleigh forget her unhappy past?

Sometimes the sweetest passions can be found right next door, or literally on your doorstep, as in Elizabeth Sites's touching story *Stranger in Her Arms* and the fun-filled *Bachelor Blues* by favorite author Carolyn Zane.

Natalie Patrick makes her writing debut with the heartwarming *Wedding Bells and Diaper Pins.* Winning custody of her infant godson seemed a lost cause for Dani McAdams until ex-fiancé Matt Taylor offered a marriage of convenience. But unexpected feelings between them soon began to complicate their convenient arrangement!

Happy Reading!

Anne Canadeo
Senior Editor

Please address questions and book requests to:
Silhouette Reader Service
U.S.: 3010 Walden Ave., P.O. Box 1325, Buffalo, NY 14269
Canadian: P.O. Box 609, Fort Erie, Ont. L2A 5X3

Books by Carolyn Zane

Silhouette Romance

The Wife Next Door #1011
Wife in Name Only #1035
*Unwilling Wife #1063
*Weekend Wife #1082
Bachelor Blues #1093

*Sister Switch

CAROLYN ZANE

lives with her husband, Matt, in the rolling countryside near Portland, Oregon's Willamette River. Their menagerie, which included two cats, Jazz and Blues, and a golden retriever, Bob Barker, was recently joined by a baby daughter, Madeline. Although Carolyn spent months poring over the baby name books, looking for just the right name for their firstborn, her husband was adamant about calling her Madeline. "After all, Matt plus Carolyn equals Madeline." How could she resist such logic?

So, when Carolyn is not busy changing Maddie, or helping her husband renovate their rambling one-hundred-plus-year-old farmhouse, she makes time to write.

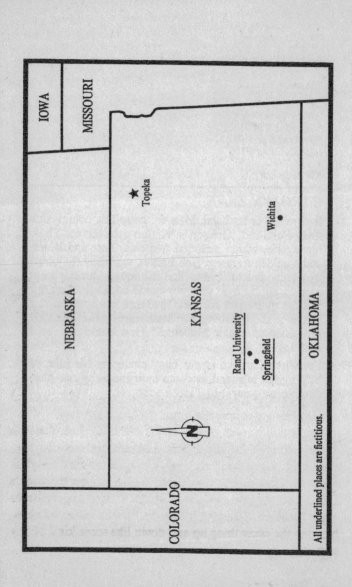

All underlined places are fictitious.

Chapter One

The sound of shattering glass and the spine-tingling crash of some unidentified falling object pulled Cole Richardson out of the deep all-encompassing concentration he had focused on his computer monitor.

What the...? His head snapping to attention, Cole decided the sounds in question had come from the front of his duplex apartment. Standing quickly, he pushed his chair away from the computer workstation in his bedroom and ran downstairs to see what on earth had happened.

In his living room, much to his disbelief, Cole found a broken-down hideously upholstered sofa bed teetering precariously in the space previously occupied by his plate-glass window. Slack jawed, Cole raked his hands over the week's growth on his jaw and stared at the absurd apparition as wind and rain slashed through the broken panes of glass, blowing the crazy thing up and down like some kind of seesaw.

Cole had heard of drive-by shootings, but this was ridiculous. Assault with a deadly piece of furniture? Why on earth would anyone attack him with a living-room set? What had he done? Stepping closer to inspect the damage, he wondered if maybe it wasn't some student he'd given a failing grade to. But why go through all the trouble of pitching a couch through his window? Wouldn't a simple rock have done the trick?

As she jerked the speeding runaway farm truck to a screeching halt mere inches before it collided with her new front porch, Lark St. Clair heard the cords that held her poor, old sofa in place on the cab's roof snap.

"Ohmagosh!" she breathed as she watched her sofa catapult over the top of the enormous flatbed truck and into the plate-glass window of her late husband's old duplex apartment building. *How in the world...?* Stunned, her mouth dropped open in astonishment.

The long, sloping yard was much steeper—and she'd been moving much faster—than she'd thought.

"Oh, well," she moaned out loud to her delighted five-year-old daughter, who sat between her and the dog in the truck's cab. "At least we don't have to carry it into the house."

How she'd ended up careening out of control and down her steep new front yard, she'd never know. She hated, hated, *hated* this stupid farm truck. It was evil. Standing on the clutch with all her weight, she battled the gearshift into reverse and bounced back up the long yard, over the curb, onto the street and into what sounded like... a car.

Running back upstairs to his bedroom to grab a raincoat, Cole knew that whoever was responsible couldn't be far away. And when he caught up with them, he'd make them sorry they were ever born.

"Ahh!" Cole groaned in frustration, as the fall thunder-shower that was raging outside his window seeped through the rotten and missing shingles on this poor excuse for a shelter and began to drip through his bedroom ceiling onto his computer. Muttering angrily under his breath, he dragged his computer table to the middle of the floor and then strode down to the kitchen for some pots and pans.

"Blasted slumlord," he spat, wedging a large pot into a corner, directly under the heaviest stream. "Doesn't give a damn whether the stupid place goes to hell in a hand basket, as long as he gets his money." Grouping three more large pots in the center of his bed, he cursed the question-able ethics of his unscrupulous landlord.

"How the devil am I supposed to concentrate with all this racket going on?" he shouted at the brown water stains on his ceiling. The echo of various water flows reverberated noisily in the metal pots, effectively drowning out his fury.

He'd been on the verge of discovering the elusive answer he'd been searching for all summer long. The answer that would unlock the door to a brilliant new technology. The answer that would make the textbook he was writing for the computer-science class he taught at Rand University go down in history as the forerunner of great things to come.

Until moments before that stupid couch had come bar-reling through his window, the answer had escaped him. Then just as the answer began to magically and mystically appear in the working subconsciousness of his mind, the sound of shattering glass snatched it from his grasp.

Someone was going to pay.

He knew his project could just possibly be one of the most brilliant discoveries to come out of this university in years. Pulitzer prize-winning material. The stuff young million-aire computer gurus were made of. He could retire at the tender young age of thirty-four.

Okay, maybe thirty-four was a little optimistic…. But for now, any bonehead Computer Science 101 student would be able to understand and design his own software after reading Professor Richardson's book.

Yeah, right. Cole plowed his hands through his hair in frustration.

Thanks to some idiot who couldn't be bothered to take his used furniture to the dump, the answer still lay just beyond his grasp. If he didn't figure this thing out soon, he'd miss the end-of-the-year deadline the university press had set to publish his book. He'd promised his department a dazzling new textbook by then, and it was a promise he intended to keep. Fall term started in just three short weeks. He was running out of time.

Yanking open his closet door he quickly riffled through his clothes, looking for his raincoat. His soggy clothing had not escaped the water works.

He'd love to tell the creep who owned this place where he could stick his lease, but unfortunately for him there was a critical housing shortage in this small college town. Kind of took the punch out of a threat to move, when he had no place to go. Some other chump would just move in anyway, happy to have even this piece of garbage housing.

No wonder the poor slob who'd lived in the duplex apartment next door for two years moved out yesterday. Cole couldn't blame him. Too bad, though. He was just the kind of neighbor Cole loved. Quiet. Kept to himself. A loner. He'd miss old what's-his-name. Probably get some party animal neighbor now, he thought irritably, heading back down to the kitchen for the rest of his bowls, glasses, cups, saucers … anything that would hold water.

Finally satisfied that he'd done everything in his power to keep the rotten building from floating away, Cole headed outside to apprehend the mad furniture vandal.

* * *

Lark yanked on the emergency brake as she fought a sudden uncontrollable flood of tears. Oh, how she longed for the mechanical ability of her late husband, Ben. He knew how to drive this demon-possessed monster. He would have known how to navigate the hundred miles from Butteville, Kansas, to Springfield without demolishing assorted mailboxes, fence posts, windows, car bumpers....

It's just that the dumb thing is so... *wide,* she thought, attempting to blink back the tears. Lark could feel her precious nest egg shrinking by the second.

Sniffing and dabbing at her nose with the sleeve of one of Ben's old oversize flannel work shirts, she turned to inspect Molly and AWOL, their large golden retriever.

"Are you all right, honey?" she queried the cheery-faced child, too afraid to get out of the truck and see what exactly it was that she had run into.

"Umm-hum. Can we get out now?" Molly was anxious to run and get a closer look at their flying sofa.

"In a minute, sweetie," she answered over the tightness in her throat. "Let me find our umbrella before you go out there in that rain. It's somewhere in the back with our furniture."

AWOL leaned over and licked her cheek, further threatening her last shred of composure. Turning off the ignition, the old flatbed sputtered, rattled, coughed and finally, groaning pitifully, died.

The heavily clouded sky lent a somberness to what was already a very depressing day, and the leaves on the trees that surrounded the old duplex were beginning to turn, signaling the return of fall. Lark hopped out into the rainstorm, ran to the back of the truck and began rummaging around for an umbrella.

"Well, Ben," she murmured to the spirit of her great redheaded bear of a man. "We made it. A little worse for the wear," she noted as she surveyed the dent she'd put in somebody's little red sports car.

This had all made so much sense from the safety of her kitchen on the ranch back in Butteville. Ben had been gone for well over a year, and she had no marketable skills other than housewife and mother. She'd been sure it was the only option. Sell the ranch, pay the obscene mountain of bills, take what was left . . . and start over.

Too bad all that was left was a little duplex Ben had owned when he was a student, in a Kansas college town over a hundred miles away. At the time, it had seemed like the perfect solution. After all, she reasoned, when life hands out lemons, make lemonade, right?

Lark ducked under the bed of the truck to avoid being washed away by a particularly heavy deluge.

What had she been thinking? she wondered, looking down the tree-lined street of the bustling college town. She didn't belong here. What made her think that she could fit in? A college, for heaven's sake. She had no business going back to school at her age. And what about Molly? How would she take care of her daughter, pass her classes and fix up this, this—she eyed the sorry-looking duplex morosely—*dump?*

The lawyer who had managed the place said it would need a little fixing up. But this?

"Aww, Ben," she moaned, and dodging raindrops she gave up on her search for an umbrella and jumped back into the cab with Molly.

It was a hundred times worse than she'd ever imagined. Peering through the rain that drizzled depressingly down her window, she polished a spot in the foggy surface and stared. Good Lord. If she'd only known, she'd have packed the wrecking ball. For there, planted before her—in all of its abject neglect—sat Ben's duplex, held up by what appeared to be a few rusty nails.

The front porch listed to the left, the house listed to the right, the roof, what was left of it, sagged sadly around a crumbling brick chimney. Great hunks of siding were missing, exposing ragged and rotten tar paper that barely covered the silvery weathered boards underneath. Blistered and peeling paint hung in festoons from the eaves and trim, and the poor gutters, rusted and overworked by the immediate rainstorm, sprayed water like a fountain in every direction.

The old place had the haunted feel of a house long abandoned and forgotten. It was truly a miracle that it hadn't been boarded up and condemned by the city.

Lark shook her head and sighed. *Ben, why did you always have to leave everything to the last minute?*

Not one to sit and lament a problem she had no control over, Lark told herself she was just overly tired and it probably looked worse than it was. Scrubbing at her watery eyes with her sleeve, she took a deep breath and gave herself a stern talking-to.

Since when had she ever backed down from a challenge? Ben always used to say she was one of the spunkiest women he'd ever met.

Smiling resignedly down at her excited and wriggling daughter, Lark said, "Well, sweetie, we're home. What do you think?"

"I think it's neat-o!" Molly cried and clapped her hands, causing AWOL's tail to slap loudly against the seat.

"Neat-o," Lark echoed, and cautioning the young girl to sit tight for a moment longer, she prepared to get out and inspect her new digs.

This was just great. In a foul mood to begin with, Cole charged into his living room and glanced around the dump—which just seemed to grow worse by the minute. The blasted landlord would probably wait at least twelve years to replace the window. How could he write anything under these conditions? He would never be able to meet his deadline. January the first loomed depressingly ahead. This project required exceptional powers of concentration and complete silence. Even the campus library was too noisy for this job. Cole could see the shining future of his innovative textbook being sucked out the window along with his stained and torn drapes.

The flames of anger flared higher in his gut. He'd get to the bottom of this, he decided, and yanking open his front door, he leapt across the crooked porch, jumped over the broken steps and landed in the middle of the cracked and sunken walkway, where he ... stopped. *What the Sam Hill?*

Not only did he have a lumpy, old couch hanging halfway through his front window, but some idiot in an immense flatbed farm truck had backed into and dented the fender of his gleaming red Porsche.

Dented, nothing, he winced, as he ran to survey the damage to his pride and joy. Crumpled, was more like it. *Great. Just great.* The flames of anger burning in his gut burst into a four-alarm fire as he ran over to the crazily angled truck, looking for the jerk who'd just turned his relatively peaceful life upside down.

Heaven help this clown when he got hold of him, Cole thought savagely, storming around the back of the furniture-filled rig. The mood he was in, he only hoped the poor slob carried plenty of dental insurance. He was going to need it.

Who was this guy? he wondered, looking in derision at the mismatched odds and ends ineptly loaded onto the back of the truck. It looked like the Salvation Army was moving in to the other half of the duplex. Wasn't it just like his slumlord to rent the apartment next door to a disreputable tenant?

Angrily rounding the corner of the truck to the passenger side he came face-to-face with a tiny, fiery red-haired child, who stood on the broad running boards and smiled up at him.

"I can't get down," she said, holding out her arms to him in a most irresistible manner.

Caught off guard, Cole stopped and stared. She was, without a doubt, one of the most adorable minxes he'd ever laid eyes on. Large, round green eyes, a peaches-and-cream complexion dotted with a sprinkling of light freckles, and dimples at the corners of her rosebud mouth. With her riot of flaming curls she resembled a live Raggedy Ann doll. Too bad she was going to have to witness her father getting beaten to a pulp.

Valiantly ignoring her outstretched arms, Cole took a deep breath. "Where's your father?" he asked, raking an agitated hand through his tangled locks.

Molly's face puckered slightly as she glanced up at the angry sky. "Up there," she said simply.

Cole looked up, expecting to see a man sitting on a rocker lashed to the top of the truck.

"Where?" he asked again, turning back to face the child.

Molly shrugged and smiled angelically. "In Heaven."

Cole glanced over at his mangled fender. Surely the child's father hadn't died in the accident, although if this display of driving were any indication... Maybe he should look under the truck.

"He lives with the angels now," she explained.

"Oh." Cole had the decency to look contrite. "Where's your mother?"

"She said she wanted to go to the apartments and see if anyone was home. She told me to stay here with AWOL, but I want to get down now." Her tone turned petulant.

A large canine head nudged the girl aside and suspiciously inspected the man standing next to the truck.

"Do what your mother says, then," he instructed the child, in his best parental voice. Clicking the door shut af-

ter she reluctantly did his bidding, he set off to search and
destroy Mommy Dearest.

Cole battled his way into the overgrown jungle that served
as his backyard and froze.

For there, standing on her tiptoes in what suddenly
seemed a tropical paradise, was the grown-up version of the
child out front. And she was ... stunning. Though her hair
was the color of midnight, it was obvious that she was the
munchkin's mother. She had the same large, expressive eyes,
this time in a shade of the deepest violet he'd ever seen, and
a flawless complexion that flushed with exertion as she
searched around for a way to climb up to his back porch.
She'd pulled her wild, curly raven hair back into a ponytail
with a large clip, but stray wisps escaped and framed her
heart-shaped face in a most appealing way. The same dimples adorned a fuller version of the rosebud lips, and her
lithe, petite figure was not completely hidden by the soft
worn flannel of her oversize shirt.

The flames continued to burn in Cole's gut, fueled now
by the celestial being who slowly turned her sensuous violet
eyes on him.

Still paralyzed, he stood, legs spread wide for balance,
arms crossed defensively across his chest, eyes narrowed
with distrust. Struggling with an inner skirmish between his
anger and his prurient interest, he valiantly attempted to
reign in his wayward libido and get back to the business at
hand.

His recalcitrant eyes strayed to her shapely legs molded by
snug, soft denim blue jeans.... The thought of his poor
bumper brought him to his senses.

"Would you mind telling me what you think you're doing?" Cole demanded, shaking off the ridiculous instanta-
neous attraction he felt toward this angel of destruction. She
was trespassing.

The tentative hopeful smile she wore faded from her lips. Eyes snapping, she took a step toward him. "I'm just looking around. Not that it's any business of yours."

Snorting in disgust, he laughed out loud. "That happens to be my back porch you're snooping around, so I guess that would make it my business."

Her face paled slightly for a brief second, then drawing herself up to her full five and a quarter feet, she glared at him. "Technically, it's not your back porch," she retorted, pushing her slender body away from the rotting railing and brushing past him on her way back to the front yard.

"Hey!" Outraged, Cole stared after her in disbelief. Just who the devil did she think she was? She couldn't just vandalize his home with her furniture, run into the car that had set him back a year's salary and then...then...give him the brush-off. "Wait just a minute," he shouted, striding quickly after her.

She was standing on the old truck's running boards, helping her daughter and that flea-bitten dust mop the kid called AWOL to the ground. The child and dog immediately hit the ground running and proceeded to find and explore every water-logged pothole the yard had to offer.

"I asked you, what are you doing here?" He continued his inquisition as he caught up to her. Please don't say moving in, he silently begged.

She smiled smugly up at him. "As I'm sure you can see, I'm moving in."

Cole's head dropped back on his shoulders as he searched the dark and brooding sky for mercy. *Why him?* "Wonderful. What are you going to do now?" he quipped, his voice loaded with sarcasm. "Toss the rest of your stuff through the window? Or perhaps you'd care to just back across the lawn and unload dump-truck style right there onto the porch?"

She scowled at him with burning reproachful eyes. "That," she declared, pointing at his front window, "was a freak accident."

Cheeks on fire, she watched her sofa bed rock lazily in his window frame. "I promise, I'll take care of that." She'd been prepared to apologize profusely and offer complete compensation from the beginning. But frankly, his attitude was beginning to tick her off.

"Sure. Right. Good luck." Cole blew a long-suffering breath from his lungs. "The imbecile who owns this place won't bother to replace the window till hell freezes over, and even then it's iffy."

"I said . . . I'd take care of it," she ground out, spinning to face him, planting her hands firmly at her tiny waist.

"Yeah, right. You."

"Yes. Me. The imbecile who owns this place."

Cole stared at her, completely nonplussed. *"You?"* he croaked. The little woman standing in front of him owned this landfill?

"Yeah. Me." Her eyes dared him to challenge that.

This just got more pathetic by the second. "You mean to tell me you're the one who's been letting this place fall down around my ears while I pay you for the privilege?"

"Don't worry. I plan on making some repairs."

"*Some* repairs? I hope you brought a couple of sticks of dynamite with you in that . . ." he jerked a thumb in the direction of her enormous truck " . . . rolling thrift store." He could tell he'd scored a low blow, as the brief flash of hurt passed across her pretty face. Now he felt bad. What was it about her that made him want to rant and rave and at the same time protect her from life's trials?

"I'm sure it's not as bad as all that," she bristled.

Cole snorted in derision. "Lady, you don't know the half of it. I've been waiting a long time to tell you just exactly how bad it is. In fact, I . . ."

"Look, buddy," she interrupted impatiently, "I didn't just drive over a hundred miles to stand out here in the rain and fight with you." She brushed the water-soaked tendrils out of her eyes and blinking rapidly tried to sneer at him.

"Well, by all means. Let's go *inside* and stand in the rain and fight." He waved his arms wildly in the direction of his apartment. Her dog came to sit protectively in front of its master, a low growl deep in its canine throat.

"Will you back off?" Her eyes glittered with purple sparks of anger as she poked a finger into his chest. "I said I'll take care of the repairs."

The dog growled again, and looked up at its master for what Cole feared would be the command to kill. Oh, big deal. At this point he was beyond caring.

"I don't suppose some of those repairs you're planning would include my bumper?" His voice rose vehemently.

She squared her shoulders with pride, and stepping around her dog came nose to neck with him. "I... have...insurance." She spit each word as if it were a bullet and his Adam's apple, the target.

"I sure as heck hope so," he ground out through the spastically jumping muscles of his jaw. Narrowing his eyes, he waggled a finger in her face. The face that was now so close he could see his reflection in her angry eyes. Could feel the warm breath on his finger. "Because you're going to need it, lady."

Her whole body tensed with fury. "Oh, blow it out your..."

"Hi."

Both heads snapped around to see who was speaking.

Randy. Cole had forgotten that his best friend was dropping by to borrow a book. "Hello, Randy." Doing his best to get a grip on his temper, Cole attempted to speak civilly.

Lark chose the opportunity to make good her escape and ran to pull her daughter out of a low-limbed tree.

"Who's the dishy broad?" Randy ambled up to Cole and inclined his tall, dark and handsome head in Lark's direction. Ever the playboy, Randy Kingman prided himself on never missing an opportunity.

"My landlord."

Randy hooted with glee. "*She's* the slumlord you're always ragging about? No way."

Cole's shoulders slumped dejectedly. "It's true. And she's moving in next door. With her kid. And her dog, no less."

Clapping Cole heartily on the shoulder, Randy threw back his head and laughed. "Just what you need." He glanced around. "What about her old man?" Turning, he watched with interest the way Lark's shapely rear end strained against the faded denim of her jeans as she hoisted her daughter into her arms.

"Her daughter tells me he went to live with the angels."

"That's too bad," Randy said distractedly.

Something about the way his friend was looking at his landlord irked Cole. She was the enemy. Couldn't this overgrown hormone see that?

"So, what's she like?"

"How on earth should I know?" Cole barked irritably. "She's a lousy driver." He pointed to his shattered window and then at his flattened bumper.

"Holy... She did *that?*" Bug-eyed, Randy stared at Cole's new window seat, then moved over to inspect the damage to his car.

"Yep." Cole followed his friend to the curb.

Lark could feel the hostility radiating toward her from clear across the yard, as she helped Molly down to the ground and suggested that she go explore the backyard. Scampering happily to the other side of the house, Molly's voice grew faint as she sang.

"Bringing in the sheets, bringing in the sheets. We shall come when Joyce rings...."

Lark's mouth curved indulgently until her eyes drifted to Mr. Friendly, her new tenant and neighbor. What was it about this man that had her hackles standing at attention from the very second she first caught sight of those baby blue eyes?

She didn't have much experience with men, but she knew she'd never reacted to Ben that way. They had always gotten along just fine, even when Ben was busy hustling up some impossible get-rich-quick scheme or another. Rarely had a cross word passed between them. No. Ben had never, in their entire marriage, made her feel the anger... the frustration... the humiliation that her new neighbor/tenant had made her feel within the first minutes of meeting. Ben had never made the little hairs at the back of her neck stand on end when he'd raked his eyes over her body either. But then Ben hadn't been much into raking with his eyes....

Walking over to her truck, Lark attempted to ignore the two men who stood shaking their heads over the tiny dent in his fancy, little bumper. For pity's sake. It had been an accident. They were making her feel like some kind of criminal. Well, her tenant was, anyway. His friend was laughing his head off—at least *he* had a sense of humor.

Lark grinned as she busied herself with unfastening the cords that held her furniture in place. Hoisting herself up to the large wooden-planked bed of the truck, Lark slowly coiled each rope and tossed them over the pile that made up her life and down to the ground. The low murmur of male voices filtered up to her from behind the truck.

She could feel Randy's frankly interested stare follow her movements and instinctively knew that he found her attractive. But she had the feeling that the darkly handsome man found many women attractive. Randy, she decided as she worked, was the type of guy a girl had to look out for. A smooth talker who could steal and break your heart. However, it would probably be fun while it lasted, she mused, listening to him laugh and poke fun at his irritated friend.

Her fair-haired neighbor, on the other hand, seemed completely different. More down to earth, centered, mature, stubborn... Pigheaded, she fumed, coiling the rope faster and faster around her arm. Too bad those golden-boy looks were wasted on such a jerk.

His long, wavy, gold-streaked blond hair looked as if it hadn't been cut in well over a year. And didn't the man own a razor? If he did, he hadn't used it in at least a week. Still though, on him, the stubble looked cute. There was a sensitivity to the soft curl of his lips that—when he wasn't smirking—gave his face a strangely vulnerable boyish look. Interesting, she thought pulling a rope out from under a pile of cardboard boxes, when you considered just how insensitive he really was.

Yes, she supposed he was probably the campus heartthrob. However, Lark didn't care if he were the best-looking guy this side of the Rockies, he was a horse's behind.

As she worked, she wondered why someone who was obviously in his late twenties or early thirties was still in school. From the look of him, she guessed he was probably one of those professional students. The type who changed his major every three to four years whether he needed to or not. But then again, who was she to criticize? At twenty-nine, she wasn't exactly a spring chicken herself.

As she yanked on the stubborn rope that seemed to be caught on something at the back of the truck bed it suddenly gave way. The sound of discordant piano notes and splintering wood—mingled with the crashing of windshield glass and Randy's howls of laughter—told Lark that if she had any hope at all of staying alive, she should start to run.

Chapter Two

"Put me down!" Lark shrieked, as she felt herself being hauled off the back end of the flatbed and into Cole's strong arms. Terrified, she struggled against him with all her weight.

"No," he grunted, gripping her tightly and running with her out to the middle of the street.

There they stood and watched with a gathering crowd of onlookers in morbid fascination as an avalanche of her worldly possessions slid off the slanting truck bed, bounced off what was left of Cole's car and landed on the ground.

Cole slowly released his grip and let her slide down his body. "Way to go," he sighed, looking for some sign of his poor car under the mountain of antiquated paraphernalia.

She was as horrified as he was, but she'd be darned if she'd show this unfeeling clod. Besides, her grandmother's piano had surely suffered as much as his precious car.

"Oh, yeah," she cried. "Like I did it on purpose!" She

wrestled her way out of the arms that still held her loosely around the waist.

"Lady, you don't have to have a purpose. You're just a natural disaster, waiting to happen. How very fortunate for me that you chose to happen here," he said caustically. Why had he bothered to save her shapely little butt just then? he wondered, marveling at her lack of gratitude.

"Oh . . . go *jump in the lake!*" she yelled up into his face and promptly burst into tears. "Y-y-you don't need to worry about m-m-me any more, because," she blubbered incoherently, "as far as I'm concerned, you're *evicted!*"

The crowd that had gathered oohed and ahhed appropriately.

"You can't evict me. I haven't done anything," Cole shouted at her retreating back. "Besides," he raised his voice as she disappeared into her side of the duplex, "if anyone is going to take legal action around here, it's going to be me."

Randy, who up until now seemed to have thoroughly enjoyed the whole spectacle, turned reproachful eyes toward his hotheaded friend. "Ah, c'mon, man. Don't you think you're being a little hard on her? Geez, Cole. It's not like she did any of this on purpose. Give her a break."

"I'll give her a break, all right," Cole said in exasperation.

Randy shook his head. "I'm going to go see if I can help her. I'd recommend that you give yourself some time to cool off before you try to talk to her about your car." With those sage words of wisdom, Cole's best friend headed into the pit after the she-devil.

"Give her a break," he muttered, stomping back into his naturally air-conditioned apartment. He was the one who needed a break here. Flopping down into his soggy easy chair, he battled a feeling of doom that settled over him like one of the rain clouds from outside. Oh, how he longed for the good old days of peace and solitude, with what's-his-name from next door. He wasn't much to look at, but at least he was quiet.

And as physically attractive as he found his new neighbor—little Ms. What's-her-name—it was definitely hate at first sight.

Lark looked up to find Randy standing awkwardly in the middle of her empty and leaking living room. Molly had already cavorted happily through the house and was back outside chasing the dog.

"He didn't mean it," he said gently, crossing the squeaky wooden floor to sink down beside her. "It's just that he's been under a lot of pressure lately. And, well, Cole's just not used to working under an attack of flying furniture." Randy's teasing tone was soothing.

She attempted to smile through her tears. So his name was Cole. "I w-was going to ap-apologize to the big jerk, b-but he was being such a meanie," she sniffed. "I mean . . . I really am sorry." Burying her head in her arms, she sighed in abject misery.

Nodding, Randy reached into his pocket and handed her a handkerchief. "Trust me. That's not like him. You'll see. He's just got a lot on his plate these days." He watched as she dabbed at her red and swollen eyes with his hankie. "So, I'm Randy Kingman. The big jerk's best friend. And you are . . . ?"

"Lark St. Clair." She held out her hand. "The owner of this dump." She shook his hand and looked around disgustedly. "Randy, this hasn't been my day."

Randy grinned. "I can see that. Hey, why don't I give you a hand getting your stuff inside out of the rain? That'll make you feel a little better. There is no way you can carry all that heavy furniture inside by yourself."

"Okay." She exhaled raggedly. "At least we don't have to worry about the piano being too heavy any more." Lark grinned up into Randy's friendly face. "We should be able to carry it in half a dozen or so loads...."

It was hopeless. The solution he'd been so close to was gone for the day. Cole turned off his computer and threw a plastic tarp over the top of his workstation, just in case the bulging, waterlogged ceiling decided to explode. He couldn't think with all the racket from the street filtering in through his front window. Not to mention the anxiety he felt over the damage to his beautiful Porsche—his baby. He ran his hands over his face and, moaning, pulled his hair back away from his forehead. Maybe if he went to bed, he would wake up and discover that this whole crazy day had been nothing but a bad dream.

A force he seemed incapable of resisting drew him into his living room, where he stood and watched the endless parade of odds and ends being transferred from the pile in the street to the duplex next-door. His landlord and his best friend seemed to be having a high, old time, giggling and laughing like a couple of senseless lunatics, as they ran through the rain with her boxes and furniture.

So she thought she could evict him, he thought, watching as she struggled with a particularly large carton. Just let her try to tangle with Professor Cole Richardson. As much as he dreamed of moving out of this falling-down pile of plaster, there was no way on God's green earth he was going to move now. No way. He'd stay, just for the perverse pleasure of making her suffer. Besides, he thought disgruntledly, he couldn't move out. There wasn't another place in town to be had.

Watching as she wrestled the giant box off the truck and into her arms, he marveled at her stamina. She was strong for her size. He had to give her that much. She was like one of those ants that could carry two or three times their body weight. He shook his head. She shouldn't be doing that— she'd really hurt her back.

Cheeks flushed with exertion, she giggled at something Randy said and staggered down the crooked sloping path toward her front door. Gingerly poking his head out the shattered pane of his living room window, Cole strained to follow her progress. Nice legs. Strong. Jeans fit like a glove too, he noted, taking care to avoid a shard of glass that hovered near his throat. She had his favorite kind of figure. Slim and petite, but sturdy.

He ducked back inside his apartment as she once again headed into the rain for another load and wondered exactly what was going on under that softly faded flannel shirt. She had a firm, little waistline, that much he'd discovered as he saved her from being buried alive earlier. And she was light as a feather. As soft, too...

Damn. What was he thinking? He'd sworn off these kinds of thoughts toward women a lifetime ago. This was exactly how it had started with his ex-wife, Sherry. He'd admired her from afar until he was putty in her scheming, two-timing little hands. The next thing he knew, he was engaged to be married and Sherry, well, Sherry was engaged in a hot affair with the Goody Bar Man. To this day he still cringed when one of those musical ice-cream trucks came cruising down the street.

Eventually—and he admitted now, stupidly—he'd forgiven her and they'd married at the impossibly young age of eighteen, become parents of their son, Jake, at nineteen and divorced at twenty. Sherry had hated being tied down. And at the time Cole believed the old saying, if you love something, let it go; if it's yours, it will come back....

So he had let go. Sherry had gone and taken Jake with her, leaving him devastated, alone and waiting for her return. Unfortunately she'd never come back. Instead, she'd married a wealthy older man who was happy to indulge her every whim, including adopting her young son. Cole, being barely more than a child himself, had figured it was in the best interests of the child to go along with her wishes. Besides, avoiding joint custody with Sherry meant avoiding having his heart ripped out every other weekend.

Now, much older and wiser, he knew he'd made a mistake. He should have fought for the right to parent his son. But it was too late. As much as he'd love to know his own little boy, that boy was a teen now and didn't need him.

Sighing, Cole leaned his cheek against the cool molding that surrounded his shattered window. It all seemed part of another life. A life that had taught him not to trust women as far as he could throw them. Oh, he thought, raking his hands through his overlong tangled locks, he knew that university life afforded a multitude of opportunities to search for Ms. Right, but he had no desire. When it came to love and marriage, his heart was stone.

"Mary had a little lamp, little lamp, little lamp. Its beam was kind of low..." a little voice sang out from the front yard.

Molly had fashioned a mangled wreath of flowers from the weeds in the yard and it rested askew on her wild, curly hair as she slowly threaded her way toward her mother. Smiling, Cole watched as she turned her sunny face up in the mist and missing a step stumbled to her knees in a puddle. He knew virtually nothing about little children and even less about little-girl children, but watching as Molly stood back up, he realized she was remarkably resilient. Like her mother.

Cole's eyes refocused and he was pulled from his ruminations by the sight of Randy and his landlord attempting to wrangle her ancient refrigerator freezer to the ground. What was she trying to do? Get herself killed? Cole flexed his fists in frustration. She was too small to lift that old thing. It was clearly five or six times her size and weight.

Oh, for crying out loud, he thought, rolling his eyes and planting his hands on his hips. She was going to get herself squashed if he didn't go out there and give her some blasted help.

Before he could analyze his motives, Cole was out the door, across the porch and out in the rain to once again save the darn woman. The woman who, one way or another, would surely be the death of him.

Lark was positive her back was breaking in two. She only hoped that Molly and AWOL were not hovering somewhere around her ankles, as she and Randy attempted to maneuver her forty-year-old refrigerator to the ground. Back at the ranch in Butteville, Slim and Chet had made loading the stupid thing look like a piece of cake. Why hadn't she thought to bring the hand truck with her?

Just when she was sure her fingers were permanently curled into a bent position and her arms were shrieking in agony, Lark felt herself unceremoniously nudged out of the way and her end of the burden suddenly lifted from her hands.

Startled, she looked up as Cole continued to nudge her aside and shout instructions to Randy who struggled under his end of the load. If she weren't so incredibly grateful for the respite, she'd have slugged him for his audacity. Just how overbearing was this guy, anyway? She had been doing just fine, thank you very much, she bristled, as he made lowering the old appliance to the ground look easy.

She was no fragile, coddled city girl. Obviously this hip, happening big man on campus had no idea what it took to be a farm wife and mother, or he would have let her be. She'd helped Ben muscle larger and heavier pieces of equipment to and fro without so much as a broken nail, and her late husband had been glad for the help.

Still though, somewhere down deep inside her, Lark was pleased to be treated like a lady. It had been a rare occurrence on a ranch the size of theirs. Especially since Ben passed away and it had been up to her to carry on with many of his daily chores. It was sort of refreshing to have a man interested in her physical welfare. It just felt a little strange, that's all. And a little bit wonderful, she decided as she watched Cole grapple the heavy end of the refrigerator with his well-muscled arms. For a city boy, he had a great build. She had to give him that much.

Probably spent all of his free time lifting weights in one of those expensive gyms. Keeping that carefree beachboy image of his finely tuned...

What was she doing? It was clear that she'd been a grieving widow for so long that any pretty face, no matter how obnoxious, could turn her head. Well, she'd put a stop to this traitorous train of thought now. No rude, crabby campus jock was going to push her around. She was capable of handling her own life and her own furniture just fine.

"Hey," Cole snapped between grunts. "Get out from under my feet, will you?" Red faced, he glared at Lark through narrowed eyes.

"What do you mean, get out from under *your* feet? I was doing just fine before you came barging in to take over." Something about Cole brought out a peevishness in her personality that she didn't even know existed before today.

Of course, today would probably have brought out the pee-vishness in Mother Teresa.

"Yeah, I saw how *fine* you were doing. Now, before I drop this thing through your rickety front porch here, may I suggest that you get the hell out of my way?"

"I'm not in your way! I'm helping."

"I don't need your help."

"And I don't need yours, either."

"Oh, yeah? Well you'll change your tune when you're in traction down at County General. Now I mean it, lady, move it, or so help me I'll..."

"Hey, uh, guys? Do you suppose you could finish your little discussion after we get this thing inside?" Randy's heavy breathing could be heard coming from the other side of the fridge.

"Oh, Randy, I'm so sorry," Lark called, and ducking under the swaying appliance, she ran to his assistance.

"Oh, Randy, I'm so sorry," Cole mimicked under his breath and rolled his eyes heavenward.

"I heard that," Lark snapped.

Cole woke at the crack of dawn the next morning to the deafening sound of hammering coming from what he believed was his living room. How could that be? he wondered, dragging his pillow over his ears.

Ooooh. Ouch. Was he sore or what? He felt as if he'd competed in some kind of boot-camp triathlon. And what was with all the commotion out front? Valiantly, he struggled to consciousness. What time was it, anyway? Sitting up in bed, he squinted at the alarm clock on his nightstand. Six in the morning. *Six in the morning?*

Oh. Right. Groaning, he fell back down on his bed as memories of the previous day came flooding back.

Lark St. Clair. The slumlord.

No wonder he felt as if he'd gone twelve rounds with the heavyweight champion of the world. He'd spent most of his afternoon—against his better judgment—battling with Lark and her furniture.

Lark. What kind of name was that, anyway? Well, it fit, if her approach to moving was any indication.

The sounds of shattering glass reached him through the heavy down of his pillow. *Now* what was she up to? he groaned to himself, as he sat up in bed and reached for a pair of jeans. As quickly as his screaming muscles would allow, he pulled on his pants and headed downstairs.

Snapping on the living room light, he came face-to-face with a large piece of plywood, now covering the gaping hole that Lark's flying sofa had left.

"Oh, that's attractive," he muttered, and smacking off the light he headed wearily back to bed.

Oh, for... Cole broke his pencil in two and threw it at the wall. Unable to get back to sleep, he'd decided to take advantage of the early morning hours and get some work done on his textbook. Laboring over the software-design problem that had eluded him the day before, he'd been sitting deep in thought and staring pensively at his computer.

Until the whine of what sounded like an electric saw broke through his concentration. What on earth? Who would be sawing? And at this ungodly hour of the morning, no less.

Pushing back his chair, he followed his ears to the wall and was not a bit surprised to discover that the commotion in question came from Lark's apartment next door. Just what the devil was she up to now?

He stood, scratching his jaw, and wondering what he should do about the noise pollution that had taken over the building. There was not an industrial-strength earplug invented that could filter out that window-rattling din.

Then just as suddenly as the ear-splitting whine had started, it stopped. Relief flooded through Cole. Maybe she was finished. At least he wouldn't have to go over and confront her. He'd had a bellyful of confrontation the day before, and the less time he spent in Ms. St. Clair's presence, the better. Tiptoeing back to his computer, as if any noise on his part would set her off again, he sat down and got back to work.

Now...where was he? Valiantly gathering his powers of concentration, Cole stared hard at his monitor. For a whole minute. Because a minute of pure golden silence was all he was allowed before she started in again. Cole sat, incredulous as he was serenaded with a cacophony of hammering, banging, clanking, whining power tools and an occasional feminine voice, talking out loud to herself.

Unable to take it any more, Cole leapt to his feet— knocking his chair over in the process—and headed next door to put a stop to this insanity.

Bounding across his front porch he nearly tripped over Molly, who sat eating a piece of toast slathered with peanut butter and jelly. AWOL eagerly hovering by, lapped up loose crumbs and globs of jelly from the stairs as her little mistress dropped them.

Molly smiled up at him, and holding up her sticky, dripping toast, offered him a bite.

"Uh...oh, that's okay. No thanks, kiddo." Cole grinned in spite of himself. She really was a little doll. "I came over to talk to your mama."

"She's in there." Molly held up a jam-covered finger and pointed at her front door. "I have to stay out here, cause it's dangerous in there."

Good idea, Cole mused, knowing what he did of the child's mother. His repeated pounding on the door finally roused a frazzled Lark, who greeted him with a cordless phone tucked between her shoulder and ear.

Beckoning him inside, she waved him toward a chair and whispered, "I'm on hold."

Cole, ignoring the chair, stood staring at the gaping hole in the middle of the living room floor. A large freshly cut hole that he was sure hadn't been there yesterday.

"Dry rot," she sighed to him and turned her attention to the person at the other end of the line. "Hello, Judy? Is this the Judy I order the books from? The ones advertised on TV?" She flopped down into a chair and smiled. "Yes. The home-improvement series. All of them. Plumbing, wiring, roofing, the whole ball of wax. Yes, now." Lark sat forward in the chair and frowned. "No, I can't wait that long. This is an emergency! I need the full set *now*. No. Every six weeks will be too late. No, Judy, you don't understand. In six weeks, I won't need them any more. The darn house will have fallen down by then. Sure. I can hold."

Lark looked over at Cole, who stood staring at her as if she'd grown another head. "She's talking to her supervisor. What can I do for you?" She had the funny feeling that this wasn't a social call.

"What can you do?" Cole asked, as the realization that she was planning a major renovation on the old dump began to sink in. "You can knock it off with all the noise, that's what you can do."

"Sorry," Lark slumped back into her chair, "but no can do."

"No can do? What do you mean, no can do? I'm trying to write a very complex textbook, here. A task that requires peace and quiet. And I have a deadline I take very seriously," he drawled, his eyes hard. "Plus, in case you were unaware, this is a college town and school starts in three short weeks. People like to be able to study without fear of going deaf."

She watched in silence as he plowed his hands through his long golden locks. She wished he didn't look quite so appealing when he was mad.

Cole continued to rant. "So, listen up. I don't want to hear 'no can do!' I don't want to hear anything. I want complete silence. Do you understand?"

Good heavens. Lark felt the hackles that only Cole seemed capable of stirring up begin to rise. Just who was the landlord and who was the tenant here? Last time she checked, it was *her* building.

"Look, Cole, you're just going to have to get used to the noise, because it's *my* building and I decide how noisy it is around here. In case you hadn't noticed, this place is falling down around our ears."

"Well, whose fault is that?" Cole demanded as he looked around, his expression full of derision.

Lark turned her attention back to the phone. "Hello?" She glared at Cole. "Still on hold. Anyway, I think you should be grateful that I intend to remedy that little problem."

"Little problem? Lark, take off your rose-colored glasses for a second and get real. Do you have any idea what you're getting yourself into?"

Bristling defensively, she retorted, "I'm not stupid. I can learn to do anything as well as any man."

"Hey, I'm not stupid either, but you don't see me chopping giant holes in my living room floor. Just how the heck do you propose to put this back together?" He peered dubiously into the dark and foreboding crawl space under the house.

Lark blew the air from her lungs in a giant puff of exasperation. "Cole, you may as well give up. The place needs work, and I intend to work on it."

Crossing his arms belligerently over his broad chest he spun to face her, sparks of anger darting from his heavily gold-fringed eyes.

"Fine. But, I have a textbook to write, and there are city ordinances about noise pollution around here. Maybe out on the ranch you can play demolition derby till the rooster crows. But here in town you have to have some consideration."

"How about showing a little consideration for me then, and letting me get back to work." Lark wasn't about to be pushed around by this overgrown undergrad.

At the end of his rope, Cole yanked open her front door and fired his parting shot over his shoulder. "Fine," he barked. "Get back to work. Consider this my thirty-day notice." And with that he stepped over Molly and the dog, and bursting through his apartment viciously slammed his door shut behind him.

"Fine," Lark crabbed, as she heard—and felt—Cole's slamming door. "Let him move out. He can just drop dead for all I . . . Judy? Yes, I'm still here. You can? Great! That soon? Wonderful. Yes, I can hold. . . ."

Lark settled back in her chair and studied the hole in her floor with apprehension. Cole had a good point. How was she going to put the floor back together? She hadn't thought that far ahead. Oh, well. That's what these books were for. They'd have all the answers.

Judy came back on the line and finished taking her order. That done, Lark sighed and tossed her cordless phone on a pile of boxes.

Mr. High and Mighty next door could just watch her dust. Dammit anyway, she could make as much noise as she wanted. It was her house, after all, not his. He was acting as if he owned the darn place—and her, too.

Well, tough luck, buddy. Striding to the middle of her floor with determination, she picked up Ben's old saw. As she pushed the button, it roared to life with a satisfying, ear-piercing scream. Smiling, Lark jumped into the hole and continued to cut the dry rot out of her floor.

"Can you hear that?" Cole demanded, holding the phone up to the wall so Randy could hear what he was talking about. "See what I mean? And it's been going on for hours."

Randy's chuckle danced across the line. "Aw, don't worry. She'll fizzle out. Mark my words. I never met a woman who could single-handedly remodel a house from a set of books." He grew thoughtful. "Come to think of it, never met a man who could do it either. Let's face it, Cole, she's bitten off more than she can chew with this thing. Just give her enough rope to hang herself, and then you can get some work done."

The thundering roar of a saw vibrated the pictures that hung on Cole's wall and nearly drowned out Randy's voice.

"Yeah, I've got a rope she can use, too. And at this point, I'd even offer to assist her."

"Easy, buddy," Randy laughed.

What was that? "Hang on a sec, Randy." Cocking his head, Cole held the phone away from his ear and listened. Over the explosion of noise coming from next door, he could swear he heard the tiny sound of a child crying. Unable to see through the plywood that now covered his window, Cole carried the phone to the front door and looked out.

Molly, red faced and crying, was lying on the sidewalk with a skinned knee. AWOL's slobbering attempts at first aid were unappreciated as Molly screamed and pushed the dog away.

"Randy? Gotta go," Cole told his friend in a rush. "The kid fell and scraped her knee. She looks pretty upset. Listen, I'll call you later...." he said, and without waiting for an answer he tossed the phone on his couch.

The connection still good, Randy's voice buzzed across the line. "Sure, buddy." He chuckled. "I always say the way to a woman's heart is through her kid." Laughing, he hung up.

As Cole tore down the stairs to the sidewalk, Molly held out her chubby arms to him and cried so hard she could barely breathe. His heart melted instantly at her pitiful look and he quickly bent down and gathered her up to his chest. She clung tightly to his neck and proceeded to soak his shirt with tears and drool, as he murmured soothing words of comfort.

Her incoherent blubbering brought on an intense rush of paternal feelings that Cole hadn't experienced for years. Feelings that made him want to protect this particular child from everything from the bogeyman to her first date. She was still just a little baby, he marveled, looking down at the chubby knee that sported a rather painful-looking scrape. Carrying her over to the porch, he set her down.

"Do you like lemon drops?" he asked, wiping clumsily at her tears with his shirttail.

"Y-yes," she hiccuped.

"Me, too. Sit here for a second and I'll go get us some." Gently, he pried her sticky fingers from the collar of his shirt and dabbed at her runny nose with his sleeve. Rushing into the house, he grabbed the first-aid kit out of his medicine cabinet and then raided the candy dish on his coffee table. "Here," he said as he returned and popped a drop between the puckered drooling lips.

She watched in fascination, as Cole cleaned and doctored her knee, speaking slowly and softly to her the entire time.

"I suppose your mama couldn't hear you cry over all the racket she's making in there. But that's okay," he soothed. "I heard you." He smiled and patted her head. "If she could stop her Bob Villa impersonation for five minutes, maybe she could be out here handling this. She's just lucky she has me for a tenant, though. Right?"

Molly rewarded him with a watery grin and nodded.

He knotted the bandage securely at her knee and patted her head. Cole thought of his own son, realizing some other man had had the honor of patching the boy's scrapes.... He regretted that until this minute he'd never known how good it could feel to bring a smile to a tearful face.

"I can count backward," Molly informed him.

"You can?" This didn't surprise him. He had a feeling she was a gifted child.

"Yes. Want to see?"

"Sure." Cole smiled as Molly stood up and turned her back on him.

"One ... two ... three ..."

Lark stopped sawing. Even with the vibrating roar of her power tool, it seemed entirely too quiet. Something was wrong, her mother's intuition told her. Stepping out onto the front porch she discovered Molly, her back toward Cole, counting her heart out. Odds and ends from a first-aid kit lay strewn about and Lark could see that her coldhearted neighbor had thawed long enough to help her daughter. And she was grateful.

"Leventeen, nineteen, forty, twelve ..." She peeked over her shoulder at Cole and grinned.

"Good," the teacher in him praised. "Keep going," he encouraged and leaned back against the porch railing, enjoying the simple pleasures of a crisp, sunny fall day and Molly's childish voice.

As if he could sense her presence, he turned and grinned at Lark, who stood in the doorway watching them. She blinked rapidly at the poignant picture, a silly lump suddenly closing off her throat. Maybe she'd misjudged him, she thought, returning his smile in what seemed to be a momentary truce of sorts. Maybe he wasn't such an ogre after all.

They looked so content together on the droopy, old porch, sucking on lemon drops and basking in the slanting rays of the sun. Molly's knee was draped with yards of gauze, held in place by a large, floppy bow and Cole, seeming relaxed and happy, was sprawled comfortably across the steps. Lark hadn't thought him capable of relaxing.

As Molly continued her numerical exercises, Cole winked at Lark through his lazily hooded eyes.

"She's counting backward," he mouthed up at her and grinned.

Lark felt herself blush so fiercely that she was sure even the roots of her coal-black hair turned red. Flustered by his frankly sexy smile, she nodded. "She can count upside down, too," she whispered. "But she needs a bar to hang from."

"Umm." Cole glanced in amusement at Molly.

"Thanks for patching up her knee," Lark said, awkwardly brushing a stray wisp of hair out of her face.

"No problem."

Again, the sexy, lazy grin.

Lark backed up through the rusty screen door. This guy was dangerous. Far more dangerous in his present mood than when she was at war with him.

"Come on, Molly. It's time to eat," she announced, in an effort to keep her distance. Letting the screen door bang shut, she headed back inside to the relative safety of her apartment.

Chapter Three

"But why?" Molly's little face puckered uncertainly. "I want to stay in here with you."

"We've been over this before, sweetie." Picking up a damp washcloth, Lark reached across the breakfast table and scrubbed at her daughter's milk mustache. "My How To books finally came in the mail yesterday and I'm going to fix the electricity so this old house doesn't burn to the ground. I don't have much time to get the place patched up. School starts in just a few weeks."

She looked dubiously at the pile of information spread out on the table before her. These books were supposed to make it easy. Why, then, after reading the guide to rewiring, did she feel as if she needed to be certified by the state electrical board to change a light bulb? It was much more complex than she'd thought. Meter bases, electrical panels, breakers, fuses, 12/2 with ground... Good heavens, learning to speak Cantonese would be easier.

Sighing in resignation, she grabbed Molly's chubby hands and wiped the jam from between her fingers. Well, she'd just have to be a quick study. She didn't have the money to hire an electrician, and unfortunately the current wiring situation was critical. The original wiring had obviously been done by a madman. Surely she could do a better job than the mishmash of ancient and crumbling wires that ran like a spider web through the ceiling and walls.

"But AWOL's gone." Molly pouted. "And there are no kids here."

Lark smiled sympathetically at the child. Molly was lonely for the neighbor kids back at the farm.

"Well, why don't you go look for AWOL?" she suggested, knowing full well that the dog was prone to disappearing for days but hoping that the game would occupy Molly for the time being. "You can hunt in the backyard. I'll give you a bag of cookies to share with her when you find her, okay?"

Molly began to smile. "Okay."

"All right, then. I want you to stay outside till I call you in for lunch and, honey, stay in the backyard, where I can see you. No going out in the street. We're in town now. It's different here." Lark glanced out the window at the cloudy sky. "Go get your shoes and jacket on."

"Okay." Molly hopped down from her seat at the table and ran to her room.

Pulling the guide to basic wiring across the table, Lark opened it to the table of contents and read the first pages of warning about electrical shock and death by electrocution. As she took a sip of her coffee, she scanned the chapter headings.

"Chapter One. Simple wiring—what every home owner should know." Sounds easy enough, she thought, provided you can manage to live through the pitfalls in the danger/

warning pages. Turning to page three, figure 1a, she studied the complicated drawings.

Or not, she thought, looking at the diagram in dismay. This would definitely take a little longer than she'd anticipated.

Cole high-fived himself over the top of his computer monitor and danced a little end-zone victory jig around his workstation. Smashing an imaginary football to the floor, he held up his arms and bowed to the audience that cheered loudly in his mind.

He'd done it.

Finally, after months of intense research and preparation, he'd captured the elusive solution that would make the world sit up and take notice of his project and the textbook that documented it. The answer had been there all along, just as he'd known. It was only a matter of finding it.

And found it he had, he thought with satisfaction, looking fondly at his computer monitor. Hot dog. It really worked.

Not that he'd had any doubt, he mused distractedly, as he searched his desk for a disk to store this little gold mine on. Couldn't take any chances with something this hot. No way.

Man he felt good. Proud. Happy. Elated. And he'd managed to do it in the eye of the Lark St. Clair hurricane. He hadn't spoken to her in several days and had no idea what was going on with all the crashing and banging and power-tool noises that came from next door. He didn't want to know. However, he wouldn't be a bit surprised to walk outside and find that she'd torn down her half of the duplex and was starting in on his. That's what it sounded like, anyway.

Hmm... Where was that new box of disks? Methodically pulling open each drawer in his desk, he searched for the fresh box he remembered buying just last month. It had to be here somewhere. He thought it had been sitting right there on top of his desk next to his computer. That's strange....

A strange buzzing and popping noise filtered into his study from the apartment next door. Cole stopped to listen for moment. It sounded like a bunch of snakes. Big, mad snakes.

Zzzzzzbbzzzsssstt. Dzzzzzzzbssssszzzzt.

What was she up to now? Cole started toward the door to investigate, and froze before he'd gone five feet. His lights went out. The motor on his refrigerator stopped growling. The soft whir of his computer went dead....

Dead. As in doornail. As in black screen. As in no more answers or formula or documentation or...*anything.*

Stunned and disbelieving, Cole stared at his silent black screen. *Good Lord. It just couldn't be. Not his research project. No. No. No...!*

Cole tore at his hair with frenzied hands. It would take weeks to reconstruct all the information that set up the formula he'd just discovered. Information that until a second earlier had been happily sitting in his random-access memory, waiting patiently to be stored to a disk. Still in shock, Cole ran to his computer and tapped it.

He hit it.

He pounded it with his fist.

"Nooo...!" he shouted in agony, beginning to freak out in earnest. This just couldn't be happening. He'd worked too damn hard—been too damn close—for this to happen.

And why had it happened?

Lark St. Clair.

Turning savagely, he glared with venomous eyes at the wall that divided their apartments. This was the straw that broke the professor's back. Roaring like a lion with a thorn in his paw, he charged at the wall and beat out his frustrations with his fists until a loose sheet of drywall broke off in his hands.

How convenient, he decided, tossing it roughly aside. Why waste time walking all the way next door to chew her out, when he could easily go through the cotton-picking wall? He knew he was throwing a childish tantrum, but something about that impulsive woman next door drove him half out of his mind.

"As long as we're remodeling, let's . . . just . . . build . . . a new doorway," he shouted, as he punished the sagging drywall on her side with a passion that only Lark seemed capable of bringing out in him.

For the love of Mike, how could she do this to him? Man, it felt good to take it out on this wall. He'd always hated this wall. Come to think of it, he'd hated the whole stupid building since the moment he'd moved in.

"Out of my way," he shouted, pummeling the wall. It wasn't long before he could feel the loosened, rotting studs begin to disintegrate, just like his textbook. Seething with indignation, he boxed the rickety, old partition until he had a nice hole going at eye level.

"What do you think you're *doing?*" Lark yelled, running down her hallway to find Cole coming through the wall. Standing on tiptoe, she leaned against the vibrating structure and peered up at her fire-breathing tenant.

"Stay right there," Cole shouted. "I'm coming through!"

"But why?" she shouted back. If he hadn't looked so out of sorts, she'd have laughed. Now was definitely not the time to laugh, she surmised, taking in Cole's explosive temperament as he battled his way into her house.

"So that I can wring your gorgeous little neck! Don't move."

"Wring my neck?" Lark looked puzzled. "What for?"

"What...for...?" Cole let his head thump tiredly against the wall. "'What for,' she asks," he howled sarcastically up at the ceiling, and backing up a few paces he implored the powers that be for patience. "I'll tell you what...for..." he shouted, poking his head into her apartment and scowling what he hoped was his most terrifying scowl. "For ruining my life. That's what for!"

As he leaned against the wall, she could see it slowly beginning to weaken. Lark backed up. He was obviously having a very bad day. Even so, something about his temper tantrum didn't really frighten her. He seemed more frustrated than vengeful. At least she hoped that was the case. If he'd really wanted to hurt her physically, she figured he could have come through the front door and finished the job by now. No, Cole wasn't a woman beater but, boy howdy, he was mad.

Still, that didn't give him the right to tear her duplex in half. Looking at the damage his conniption fit had caused her wall, she felt her own dander begin to rise. She could live without the fireworks display.

"What are you talking about?" she groused, stepping on a chunk of plaster that had just come off the ceiling to get a better view of his little show of temper.

Cole stopped, his angry face covered with plaster dust, his eyes blazing accusingly, and squinted at her. "I'm talking about months of hard work, down the tubes. I'm talking about the end of what was probably a brilliant future," he hollered, and plunged his hands through a new lower hole in the wall and reached for her. "I'm talking about blowing a gold mine out of my computer with your idiotic approach to home improvement."

Lark nibbled nervously at her lower lip as she watched Cole's flailing arms search for her body. "How do you know I'm the one who blew your computer?"

He stopped flailing and pointed a furious finger at her. "Did you or did you not turn off the electricity just now?"

Uh-oh. Taking a tentative step backward, Lark shrugged. "No," she replied, her voice barely above a whisper. "Technically not."

"Technically *not?*" he roared. "Your incompetence has just cost me a fortune."

Oh, for pity's sake, why was she always on the defensive with this guy? He acted as if she'd been born to do nothing but make his life a living hell.

"I am not incompetent," she gritted out through her tight jaws. No man was ever going to make her feel incompetent again. She'd had enough of being left in the dark with Ben. He was the king of protecting the little woman from herself, and now she was paying the price. How dare some... some... man, tell her she's incompetent.

"You can't tell me you think I did this on purpose," she yelled, and punched her side of the wall for emphasis. That felt good. Repeating the process, she pounded out some of her own frustration.

Cole snorted. "Oh, of course not. You never do, do you? You just barge happily down life's little trail, looking neither right nor left, leaving a path of destruction in your wake. Well, not any more!" He glared at her through the porthole he'd created between their apartments.

"Is that what you think?" Stepping up to the hole and bringing her nose within a few inches of his, Lark returned the glare from her side. "Then tell me why it is that until I met you I never had these kinds of problems with anyone?"

Cole raked his scraped and bloodied fingers over his jaw. "I guess I'm just lucky," he sneered, exhausted by her feminine approach to reason. He'd had just about all he could take of this ridiculous conversation. He'd had just about all he could take of Lark St. Clair. Maybe Randy would be up for a game of racquetball, and he could work off some real steam. "I'm outta here," he announced churlishly. "And while I'm gone, I want my electricity turned back on!" Pushing away from the wall, his feet tangled in the archaic wiring and he suddenly felt himself falling forward.

"Lark, get out of the way!" he shouted as a doorway-size portion of the old wall—unable to take his thrashing body weight—went down for the count. Cole found himself rolling out of control into Lark's apartment, where he finally came to a stop and—shaking his head—tried to get his bearings. A dust cloud billowed up as plaster rained from the ceiling and obliterated Lark from his view.

Dear God, he'd gone too far, he thought as he scrambled to his feet and frantically searched the haze for signs of life. If she were truly injured, he'd never be able to forgive himself. She might be a pain in the neck, but he was reasonably sure she would never maliciously destroy his personal property. It's just that she had a way of making him so mad. Madder than he'd ever been before, even at Sherry and the Goody Bar Man.

Following the sounds of her choking cough, he waved his hands to clear the air and finally found her standing in the hall, out of harm's way. Her ebony hair was gray from all the dust and chunks of plaster, her face was smudged and streaked, her eyes were sparkling with fury and to Cole she was a sight for sore eyes.

"Oh, thank God! Are you all right?" he breathed, his voice filled with relief. Grabbing her by the shoulders, he hauled her up against his chest and fervently rocked her back and forth.

"I think so." She coughed, and struggling to loosen his hold she slugged him in the arm. "You big jerk! You could have gotten me killed."

"Well." He rolled his eyes in exasperation and held her out so that he could peer into her face. "I guess that would make us even now, wouldn't it?"

"Even? You call your destroying my house the same thing as my turning off your little computer?" Clutching a fistful of his shirt, Lark attempted to draw herself up to eye level with Cole.

"Lady, this dump and that lost information aren't even in the same league, as far as value goes. I'll be delighted to fix the stupid wall, if you want to reimburse me for the millions in lost revenue you just cost me."

"Ha! Millions. That's good." Lark smirked. "Dream on, college boy."

That did it. "You know..." Cole'e eyes glittered dangerously and his fingers bit into the flesh of her shoulders as he backed her up against the wall "...you're pushing your luck here." Seething, his voice was low.

"I'm pushing my luck? Why I have half a mind to..."

Unable to finish her tirade, Lark stood helpless as Cole's kiss suddenly silenced her. As she parted her lips to protest, he took advantage of the situation and angled his mouth to fit perfectly over hers. She struggled against him for a moment, attempting to voice her objections, but Cole, tired of their endless bickering, deepened the kiss and rendered her speechless.

His kiss was hard. Tortured. Fueled by the red-hot fury that only she seemed capable of bringing out in him. The frustrations of the past hours, the past days, and even the past year converged into a melting pot of emotion that pushed him to the edge of insanity.

Like a flash fire, Cole could feel the changes quickly taking place in Lark as she began to respond to his touch and meet him halfway. He reveled in the fact that she yielded to him as he boldly tasted her, slipping her slender arms around his waist and clinging to him for support.

This was crazy, he thought, losing himself in the heat of the moment. A second ago he'd wanted nothing more than to throttle her, and now...

Groaning audibly, he pulled her farther into the circle of his embrace and threaded his fingers into the wonderful silkiness of her midnight mane of hair. It felt so natural, so incredibly right to hold her like this, that if he hadn't known better he'd have thought she'd been made in heaven just for him.

Ah. But that's where he was wrong, he realized, struggling for his sanity. She wasn't some angel, sent from above. No. She was obviously the bad fairy, sent to drive him out of his mind.

Panting, he tore his mouth from hers. The last thing on earth he wanted was to get tangled up emotionally with a woman. Especially not now. He'd been stung before and was still bitter about his divorce. No, he had to get away from her. And he had to get away now, while there was still time.

Reaching behind his back, he grasped her hands in his and pulled them around to the front of his body. The look on her face suggested nearly as much confusion and disorientation as he felt, but he couldn't allow himself the luxury of feeling sorry for her. She was slowly eroding his precious grip on the quiet, little world he'd so carefully constructed and that was a luxury he could not afford.

Drawing a ragged breath, he raked his eyes heatedly over her mouth. "I can't figure out exactly what it is about you that makes me want to burn down city hall...but you're definitely driving me crazy." He shook his head and his eyes darted to the floor. "Maybe it's the fact that when you're not destroying my house or my car, you're destroying my future. Or..." glancing back up, he searched her face and shrugged "...maybe it's your gleeful, harebrained attempts at remodeling. Then, again, maybe it's the incessant racket that I've had to live with for the last few days. Hell, I don't know."

Pushing off the wall, he backed down her hallway to the hole between their dwellings and left her standing there with a dazed expression on her face. Ready to jump out of his skin and desperately wanting to run back to her and drag her into his arms, he reached down deep into his soul for courage. The courage to resist her.

"I just know I don't have time for this," he growled, angry at himself for the way he was feeling, for the emotional riptide that threatened to drag him under. From where he stood he could see the hurt his words had inflicted, reflected in her vulnerable expression, and he felt even lower—if possible—than he had before he'd torn down the wall.

Lark drew herself up to her full five feet three inches, a mask of false bravado protecting her from the intensity of his gaze.

"Well, neither do I," she cried. "It's not like I asked you to come barging through my wall like some kind of deranged maniac." She shook her hair over her shoulders amid a flurry of plaster dust and chunks. "Now, thanks to your immature tantrum I have to fix the stupid wall," she huffed and spun on her heel so that he couldn't see the tears of humiliation in her eyes. "Go on." Marching stiffly down the hall she snatched up her hammer and began grappling with a large, unwieldy piece of plywood. "Get back to your damn computer."

Feeling as if he'd just swallowed a ton of bricks, Cole stormed back to his side of the apartment without a backward glance.

"Mama, how come you hung those boards on the wall?" Feet dangling, Molly leaned back in her chair and stared up at Lark's haphazard patch job over the hole Cole had blasted between their apartments at the top of the stairs.

Dunking her grilled cheese sandwich into her tomato soup, Lark thoughtfully followed her daughter's gaze. Good question. How was she going to explain this one?

"Well, Mr. Richardson kind of had an accident and broke through the wall, so I put those boards up for privacy." She hoped Cole was listening.

"Was he playing?" the child asked, trying to rationalize this unusual adult behavior.

"Not really." Definitely not playing, she thought to herself and lightly touched her swollen lips with her fingertips.

Still curious, Molly was not about to let the issue drop. "Did he fall down?"

"Sort of..."

Molly's large eyes viewed the ragged edges of the gaping hole that peeked out from behind the plywood's straight edges with wonder. "Did he get a Band-Aid?"

Exasperated, Lark gathered her daughter's empty lunch dishes and stacked them with her own. "I don't know, sweetheart. Come on now, I need you to go back outside and play. I still have a lot more work to do on the wiring."

"I'm going to go visit Mr. Richardson and see if he got a Band-Aid."

"No!" Lark nearly shouted and then smiled to soften the harshness of her words. "Honey, Mr. Richardson is very busy and you're not to bother him, okay?"

Molly pouted. "But there's no one else to play with."

"I'm sorry, honey. I promise, just as soon as I'm done here we'll play a game, okay?"

"Okay."

"Good. Now, scoot."

Lark hung over the edge of the roof and peeked experimentally under the eaves. Okay, she thought, gripping the gutter for support, if the lines come into the house here and the meter base is down there...and the new electrical panel has to be next to the meter base, then I need to put the new panel—she slid a little farther out over the edge to get a better look—around over there.

Trouble was, the old place had three rusty fuse boxes, all in different quadrants of the building. Heaven only knew which ones were actually hot. The How To books hadn't mentioned this particular problem.

Drumming her fingers on the roof, she glanced around, wondering where the best place to install a new electrical panel would be. *Hmm. What was that?*

Looking down at Cole's window, she could see what looked like an extension cord running over to the neighbor's exterior outlet. What on earth was so important that he couldn't wait an hour or two for her to get the power back on? To hear him talk, you'd think he'd discovered the cure for the common cold.

Well, he could rant and rave all he wanted about his precious, little project. She had her own troubles. And, dealing with his fickle libido was not on her to-do list. Her face burned at the memory of their heated kiss.

How dare he, anyway? First he came barreling through her wall like a runaway freight train, then he picked a fight with her, then he kissed her senseless, and *then*—for crying out loud—he told her that he didn't have time for that? Who asked him? she fumed. How was it that he could somehow make her feel the whole incident was her fault?

Okay, so she'd experienced a little power surge that morning. Big hairy deal. Did that give him the right to make a federal case out of one little mistake? No, she huffed to herself as she crawled on her belly over the loose and rotting shingles. No, as a matter of fact, if anyone was going to make a federal case out of anything, it was going to be...

"Aaaa...aaa...aaahhh!" The patch of shingles she was resting on suddenly gave way and unfortunately Lark grasped the rain gutter for support. Big mistake, she decided immediately—but it was too late. With a shriek of agony, the rusty metal let go of the eave and fell down to the porch roof below, taking Lark and the few remaining shingles still attached to the roof with it.

Her last conscious thought before the world went black was that if she broke anything, she hoped it was Cole's concentration.

"Mr. Richardson! *Mr. Richardson!*"

Molly's shrill scream slowly broke through Cole's concentration. Deep in thought, he was on the verge of remembering an important part of the formula that Lark had zapped, when, like a skin diver submerged in the ocean he was called to the surface.

"Mr. Richardson!"

What now? he wondered, pushing his chair back from his workstation and running downstairs to his front window to see what was the matter. Plywood. Couldn't see a blasted thing.

"Mr. Richardson!" Molly's five-year-old voice, frantic with terror, met Cole at the front door.

"What is it, little buddy?" Cole pushed open the screen door and knelt down to get a better look at the little girl's contorted expression. Tears and liquid seemed to literally squirt and leak from every orifice on her young face, and Cole'd be darned if he could make out what she was saying. "Slow down, kiddo," he instructed her, and pulled her over to the front steps where he sat her down beside him. "Now, what on earth happened to make you cry so hard?" He smoothed several stray rust colored curls out of her eyes and mouth.

"Mama... huh, huh... t-told me that I'm sahuh... posed to leave you alone, huh, huh, but I, huh, think she's, huh, huh, duh... ead!"

Duh... ead? Cole stared at the child's drooling lips, trying to read the deeper meaning in her herky-jerky words. Duh... ead. Dead? Dead?

"Dead?" He repeated and felt his heart stop at her emphatic nod. "Show me where," he demanded.

"Up there." Molly pointed skyward.

"In Heaven?" Oh, good Lord, it was worse than he'd thought.

"No," she blubbered. "The roof."

What on earth was she doing up there? Cole wondered as he leapt down the stairs and sprinted out to the sidewalk to see what the kid was talking about. Sure enough, lying on the porch roof in one of the most frighteningly precarious positions he'd ever seen, was his foolhardy landlord.

Not wasting any time wondering how or why she'd got there, Cole jetted back to the porch, and scooped the wailing Molly up into his arms as he went. He dashed through the house, deposited Lark's daughter on the broken-down sofa bed—with instructions to stay put until he called her—

and took the creaky lopsided stairs three at a time, flying faster than a speeding bullet through Lark's room to the porch roof.

His heart raced, not from the effort of running up the stairs but from fear. And his greatest fear was that Molly had been right. Opening the bedroom window, Cole leaned out and looked for Lark. She lay so quietly that as he slowly made his way across the slippery porch roof he began to wonder if it was indeed his noisy landlord. Still and white as a porcelain doll, she was sprawled dangerously close to the edge of the roof and her right arm and leg dangled slowly in the air.

A nameless terror grabbed hold of Cole's heart and squeezed. How was he going to get her down from here? Maybe he should call for help. No. There simply wasn't time. Had she touched the power lines? What if she needed CPR? He hoped not. He was pretty rusty at first aid. A thousand conflicting emotions tortured him as he carefully made his way over to where she was.

"Honey, don't move," he whispered, not wanting to startle her and perhaps send her over the edge. "Lark, honey, it's me. Cole. Can you hear me?"

A muffled moan came from under the sable curtain of her wild locks.

Oh, thank God. Cole inched his way over to her body and wondered what he should do next. Flooded with relief, he fought the urge to pull her into his arms and kiss her soundly. Instead, he reached out and smoothed her hair away from her face.

"Lark, where does it hurt? Can you tell me?" He continued stroking her soft, warm cheek. "Honey, can you open your eyes?"

"Oooo." Lark's eyes fluttered open and she stared in confusion at Cole. "Where are we?"

Glancing around, Cole searched for the safest route of escape for them both. "On the porch roof."

"The porch roof?"

"Just barely. Don't move."

Lark blinked rapidly to clear her head and looked around. "Oh, that's right, I was up on the roof to get a look at the wiring situation." She winced. "Owww. It's lucky we have a porch roof."

"Well, it's lucky it didn't fall apart when you fell on it. Now that you've seen the wiring situation, maybe you'll keep your attractive little rear end down on the ground, where it belongs."

Lark ignored the sexist comment. "No way. I need to re-shingle this place." She reached under her stomach and held up a loose mossy shingle for his inspection. "This is one of the good ones."

"Oh, for Pete's sake, can't you hire someone to do that? Someone who does that stuff for a living?"

"Can't. Don't have the money."

"You won't have anything if you go and get yourself killed. I mean it, Lark. This is the last time I'm going to rescue you."

"Who asked you?" she huffed, grimacing in pain as she tried to sit up. "I don't need you to save me."

Cole snorted and rolled his eyes at that. "Okay, fine. So, you won't mind if I leave now?"

"No! I mean... please don't." Lifting her head, Lark glanced down at the ground below. It seemed much higher at this angle. She reached out and grasped his hand for support.

Cole looked down at the small feminine hands he held in his and wondered at the strength they possessed. They were capable hands, and as much as he hated to admit it she was making progress of sorts. The old place was starting to look a little better. Barely visible to the naked eye, but at least she was doing something.

"Do you have any sharp pains anywhere? Do you think maybe you have any broken bones?"

"I don't know. I feel like I've been run over by a steam-roller. My head aches, but I don't think I broke anything."

"Good, let's get you inside." Reaching down, Cole gently turned her over, away from the edge of the roof and into his arms. He supported her against his chest, and as slowly and carefully as he could, he transported her back toward her bedroom window. The going was made especially difficult by the slick, uneven surface of the roof. But Cole, operating on adrenaline and fear for Lark, carried her up to the window where he settled her before jumping inside. "Hang on," he instructed as he ran to her bed and arranged pillows and blankets for her comfort.

Abandoning his earlier resolve to remain strong and stay away from the mysterious vacuum created by Lark's violet eyes, Cole forgot all his anger and animosity toward her, and ran back to the window to lift his fragile bundle to safety.

A woman like her needed a bodyguard twenty-four hours a day, he huffed to himself, as he carried her toward the bed. He had a feeling that there would never be any controlling her, and the man who ended up with her would have to adopt the old "if you can't beat 'em, join 'em" credo. As he gently set her on the bed's edge, he wondered about Molly's father and how he'd ended up in heaven. He only hoped it wasn't from saving this minx from one of her harebrained schemes.

Helping Lark under the covers, he took in the dark circles under her eyes and frowned. She'd been working too hard.

Lark gripped Cole's arms for support against the pain in her midsection as he lowered her back against the pillows.

"All right?" Cole asked. Concerned, he sat down beside her and cradled her while she made herself comfortable.

"I think so... thanks to you."

She smiled up at him, and Cole could feel his heart turn to mush. Against his will, his eyes strayed to that rosebud mouth, framed by those incredible dimples, and back up to her mesmerizing eyes, feeling himself fall into the violet vortex of her soul all over again.

Without conscious thought of the consequences, Cole leaned forward the few inches necessary to take her face between his battered hands. Slowly, he traced the contour of her full lower lip with the pad of his thumb and watched with primal male satisfaction as her eyes betrayed her reaction. He smiled softly at the color that crept up her neck and stole into her cheeks. She was different. Neither smooth nor sophisticated like Sherry, but innocent. Sweet. Oh, so incredibly sweet, he decided as he lightly brushed his lips across hers and felt her swift intake of breath.

Knowing he was making the mistake of his life, and somehow unable to help himself, Cole abandoned all caution and drowned in the magic of the moment.

Chapter Four

Lark fell back against the pillows, drawing Cole down with her as she went. It was happening again, she thought hazily, bunching Cole's soft hair into a silky rope at the nape of his neck.

Such an odd combination of emotions. On one level, developing a physical relationship with her pompous, arrogant man-about-campus neighbor was the last thing on earth she wanted to do. After having lived with a less than trustworthy man for so many years, she was ready to swear off men altogether and make her own way in the world.

However, on a completely different level, she couldn't think of anything she'd rather be doing at this moment.

Cole's mouth sought hers—greedy, demanding, exciting. She twisted against him, attempting to seek better knowledge of a man who, oddly enough, she almost felt she'd known forever. It was as if somehow, in him, she recognized a kindred spirit. Someone who'd experienced a great deal of hurt in the past and had never quite come out the other side.

His hands roamed lower, exploring the soft lines of her waist, pulling her more firmly into his body, and Lark snuggled against him, twining her legs with his. Exploring the light stubble on Cole's cheeks with her fingertips, she shifted to allow him access to her jaw, her neck, the hollow of her throat. She ran her hands lightly down to his shoulders and explored the solid muscles she found there, thrilling at their power.

It had been so long since she'd been this close to a man. She sighed and listened to the frenzied roar as her heart beat in cadence with Cole's ragged breathing. The raw physical pleasure he brought to her was almost unbearable.

Why was it that the more they tried to keep each other at bay with their constant bickering, the more tangled their lives seemed to become, she wondered, as their hungry bodies moved ever closer together. Maybe keeping him at arm's length wasn't such a good idea. Then, again, maybe it wasn't such a bad idea either, Lark mused, shocked at her own eager response to the incredibly alluring demand of his kiss.

She knew they had to stop. This wasn't right. She'd made a vow to stay away from this particular pitfall. When Ben had died, her eyes had been open to just how stupidly naive and trusting she'd been. After his funeral, she'd consciously shut down her emotions and hadn't allowed anyone to tamper with the protective wall she'd built to surround herself. Until Cole.

Cole Richardson, the man who'd both literally and figuratively broken through the barrier to her long frozen heart. No one had ever made her feel so incredibly angry or so deliriously elated before in her life. Not even Ben.

"Mama?"

The tiny childlike word filtered into her subconsciousness, confusing her.

"Mama?"

This time the plaintive, tearful word reached her conscious mind and Lark, fighting through the haze of Cole's mind-numbing kiss, tore her mouth from his.

"Cole," she whispered, her voice dazed, breathy.

"Hmm?" Cole answered incoherently and traced the fullness of her lower lip with his tongue.

She smiled, as he drew her lip into his mouth and nibbled. "It's Molly."

"Umm." He nodded slightly. "What about her?"

Lark stilled his persistent exploration by drawing back and cupping his face in her hands. "She's coming upstairs."

"Uh-oh." Kissing her hard one last time, Cole leveled himself to a sitting position and ran his hands over his face in an effort to clear his mind.

"Mama?"

"In here, honey," Lark called and struggled to sit up.

Molly came tiptoeing into the room, her face streaked with tears. "Are you still alive?" she asked, standing in the doorway and watching as Cole sprang from the edge of the bed.

Molly's innocent question brought reality crashing back.

"Oh, honey." Lark held her arms out to the frightened child, suddenly ashamed. How could she have put Molly through the agony of wondering if she'd lost another parent? And for what? To dally with a strange man she didn't even think she liked. Feeling stupid and selfish, she reached for the child's hand. "Mr. Richardson helped me get down from the roof and put me in bed because I was feeling a little... woozy," she explained. Her face went hot as she felt, rather than saw Cole's grin.

"Did you fall down?" Molly asked, stepping into the circle of her mother's arms.

"Yes, I did," Lark answered ruefully, and ruffled her daughter's hair.

"Did you get a Band-Aid?" Molly looked up in awe at her mother's savior and grinned winsomely.

"Not yet. But I think I could use one on my elbow, don't you?" She held her bruised and scraped arm up for Molly's curious inspection. "Why don't you run to the medicine cabinet and get me one?" she suggested, and smiled as the child eagerly ran to comply.

When they were alone again, Cole fidgeted and rubbed his jaw. "Well, I can see that you are in capable hands now. So, I guess I'll just be on my way."

For some perverse reason, Lark was depressed by Cole's sudden need to escape. She knew she should be relieved that he wanted to go, leaving her to chalk up the whole sordid incident as just another accident between their lips.

Cole shifted from one foot to the other, and finally began backing to the door. "I'll just let myself out. I really have to get going."

I know, I know, she thought grumpily. You hate to kiss and run. "Yes, I'm sure I'll be fine now." She smiled to hide the mortification she felt at being foolish enough to allow herself to be tempted twice in the same day. With her tenant no less. What a fool.

"Thanks," she chirped breezily, and waved at his retreating back.

Obviously she had a few things to learn about life away from the ranch, she thought with renewed humiliation at the memory of their heated kiss.

Cole stumbled down Lark's squeaky stairs, as if one step ahead of the devil himself. He had to get out of her apartment. She had some sort of power over him that had him behaving so strangely he didn't recognize himself any more. Bewitched. That was it. She'd bewitched him with some raven-haired spell he was unable to resist.

Good thing the kid had come back when she had, he thought, bursting out her front door and breathing in great gulps of fresh air. As it was, he'd had to marshal all of his resources to tear himself out of her room.

Get a grip, man, he commanded himself, as he bounded down the porch steps and into the yard where he shadow-boxed off some pent-up energy. Got to nip this thing in the bud, Cole decided, prancing toward the side yard, practicing his right cross on the rosebushes that struggled to grow there.

"That's right. Shake her off, buddy." He barked advice to himself, as he threw a series of left jabs at the side of the house. "You don't need the aggravation. You have much bigger fish to fry. You have a textbook to wriiiieeeah . . ."

Cole felt his oxygen supply suddenly cut off as he shadowboxed his way into the extension cord he'd strung from his computer to the neighbors' exterior outlet earlier that day. As he bounced off the taut surface, the cord came unplugged, once again destroying the painstaking steps he'd made toward recovering his lost gold mine of information. This just wasn't his day.

The next day, Cole puttered at his desk, preparing for the fall-semester classes that would start in just over a week. He hadn't been able to concentrate on his book since his last run-in with Lark, so he'd given up, hoping these mundane preparations would pull him back to earth. It was strangely silent over at Lark's place and he spent part of his conscious thought wondering if she was home, or if she'd managed to finally do herself in with one of her insane renovation schemes.

Maybe he should go over and check on her.

Maybe not.

Forcing himself to concentrate on something other than the amazing beauty of her violet eyes and the sensuous explosion that happened between them every time their lips met, Cole reached under his desk for his soft leather briefcase. His hand groped around in frustration, until finally deciding it had fallen over he got down on his knees and peered around on the floor. It was soft and lumpy, so he supposed it could have slithered down behind the desk, but after a thorough examination he discovered that it simply wasn't there.

That was funny. He remembered putting it there just yesterday. He always put it there. Always. That way, he could always find it. Simple.

What wasn't so simple was the fact that ever since Lark St. Clair had come catapulting into his life, he'd been out of whack. Sighing, Cole scratched his head and let his eyes scan the rows of shelves that lined his study. No sign of the soft leather case.

He was losing his mind. Not just over the missing case but over his sexy, luscious, nutty, completely mesmerizing landlord. If the truth were known, he hadn't been able to get her out of his mind ever since her hideous sofa had landed in his living room. And now that he'd had a taste of heaven in her arms, he was more distracted than ever.

He'd never been this messed up over a woman before. Not even Sherry. Oh, Sherry had done a number on him all right, but this was different. Somehow, Lark had managed to draw him kicking and screaming into her broken-down web and then hypnotize him and hold him captive to her charms. And the trouble was, he didn't think she even realized what she was doing to him.

Not like cold, calculating Sherry. No, as much as he hated to admit it, Lark and Sherry seemed worlds apart in their approaches to life. Where Sherry was ruthless, stopping at nothing to get what she wanted, Lark was willing to work hard and make do with what she had.

But could any woman really be trusted? Cole stood, pushed his hands deep into his pockets and sighed. Oh, for crying out loud. Why was he even bothering with this ridiculous train of thought? He didn't even know this woman. She was probably just as big a schemer as Sherry. Besides, he didn't need or want a woman at this point—especially not the hellcat next door. It was all he could do to keep her from killing herself and still manage to have some time left over to work on his book.

When he got ready to start another relationship, it would be with someone he could be in the same room with for more than ten minutes without wanting to turn her over his knee. Someone he could trust.

Sighing with futility over the chaotic state of his life, Cole decided to call it a day and head for a nice, cool, mind- and body-numbing shower.

Wincing, Lark tossed the home guide to wiring down on the coffee table and reached for the book on plumbing. Her ribs still hurt like the dickens from her fall. Maybe she'd give the electrical problems a rest for a while, just until she could figure out what to do about installing a new circuit panel and hooking it to a new meter base.

Besides, if she were honest with herself, she'd have to admit that she was in way over her head. She had the sinking feeling that it was time to bite the financial bullet and hire an electrician. It beat getting herself killed. Although, when

she thought of the smug "I-told-you-so" look she was sure
Cole would render, she balked. She hated to give him the
satisfaction. Especially since that exercise in humiliation
she'd received from him the previous day. It was bad enough
to be pulled to safety like a naughty little kid, but then to be
kissed and run away from... Well, it was more than her
fragile ego could stand.

On the other hand, she was beginning to wonder if she
would ever be able to make heads or tails out of the confusing information on the wonderful world of electricity. It was
all so mysterious. Volts, amps, watts, circuits.

Frowning, Lark thumbed through the plumbing book.
This didn't look nearly as complex. Or dangerous. As she
read, she began to feel fairly confident that she could tackle
a few simple plumbing problems. How bad could it be? Re-
placing a few pipes shouldn't be any big deal.

"Hmm..." As she pinched her lips between her forefin-
gers, her brow formed a straight line and she dubiously
studied the opening chapters. "Before beginning any
plumbing project, turn the water off at the main."

Sounded simple in theory. Too bad she didn't know where
her main was. No problem. Had to be around here somewhere.

"Molly," Lark called. Gingerly climbing off the lumpy
surface of the sofa, she went to the bottom of the stairs and
stood listening to her daughter's slightly befuddled rendi-
tion of the teapot song.

"I'm a little peacock, short and stout. Here is my feather,
don't pull it out...."

"Come on, honey, we're going on a treasure hunt," Lark
said to her daughter.

A fiery mop of hair popped out into the upstairs hallway. "We are?" Beaming, Molly ran to the landing, held

tightly to the railing and clomped noisily down the stairs. "Where?"

Lark shrugged and grinned at her enthusiastic child. "Good question. I'm sure we'll know it when we see it." She held up a picture in the plumbing book. "It should look something like this." She pointed at the red-handled valve in figure 2*b*.

"Okay," Molly cried, and tore out into the backyard to search for the main at the end of the rainbow.

"I'm a little teapot, short and stout," Cole bellowed at the top of his lungs as he poured a handful of shampoo into his hand and lathered up his hair. Where had that come from? he wondered, tossing the shampoo bottle to the shower floor and continuing to hum the catchy little tune. "Here is my handle..." He waved his arms around in the age-old pantomime. Lathering up his washcloth, he turned off the spray of tepid water and attacked his upper body with mountains of soap bubbles.

"Don't pull it out..." he warbled. That couldn't be right. How did that song go, anyway? Never mind. The kid would probably know. She was a sharp little thing.

Cole grinned to himself as he resoaped his washcloth and tackled his legs and feet. Nothing like a nice lukewarm shower to relax a man and take his mind off his...neighbor. Eyes stinging from the mounds of shampoo that dripped from his head onto his face, Cole groped blindly for the faucet handle so that he could rinse.

A rusty orange stream belched from the old pipes into the shower, and holding his breath Cole stepped beneath the weak spray to rinse his soap-filled eyes. The normally weak spray of rusty water suddenly became a weak drizzle of rusty water, then a trickle and then...nothing.

Fumbling toward the wall, Cole felt for and found the faucet. Twisting it this way and that proved fruitless, except for the last dying gasp of the pipes as they struggled to produce a drop of water. He pounded the wall experimentally. Still nothing.

This had to be the handiwork of Lark St. Clair. Couldn't he even take a cold shower to get away from that woman?

"No," he huffed. She had to go and mess up even that simple pleasure. Eyes shut tightly against the blinding sting of soap, Cole stumbled angrily around his shower, tangling with the shower curtain as he attempted to escape.

He knew he had a towel around here somewhere.... He'd left it just outside the shower on the floor. Groping blindly, his hands came in contact with a great slobbering, panting body of hair. AWOL. And as far as he could tell, she was lying protectively on his pile of fresh towels. Cole felt his blood pressure rise. Was there no escaping Lark or her mutt?

AWOL affectionately kissed his fingers as he attempted to extricate a towel from under the furry body. Thinking it was all a big game for her benefit, AWOL stood, gripped the other end of the towel in her jaws and shook her head playfully back and forth.

Squinting through the eye that was in less pain, Cole reached out and gripped the towel rack to keep from being pulled off his feet.

"Hey," he yelled at the dog, hoping his tone was authoritative. Although just how authoritative he sounded—as he stood there nude and blind, playing tug-of-war with Lark's hellhound—remained to be seen.

"Stop. Sit. Stay," he commanded, searching for a word, any word that would have an effect on this growling pile of hair. Slipping and sliding around his bathroom floor, Cole clung to the towel rack, which unfortunately decided to come off in his hand.

"Dammit," he howled, waving the disconnected chrome in the air. Immediately, the dog dropped the towel and cocked her head quizzically up at him.

"Yap!" AWOL sat at his feet and wagged her tail.

Cole whipped the towel up before the game could continue and proceeded to rub the soap out of his eyes.

"So, I see we speak the same language." His words were muffled by the towel. "Good. Because right now..." he glared at the dog and fastened the terry cloth around his soapy hips "...I'm going next door to give your owner the same message." Flinging the chrome bar into the shower, he marched out of the bathroom, AWOL hot on his trail. He was too angry to stop and think about his resolve to stay completely away from Lark.

Lark turned the handle of the water main over in her hand and stared at it in dismay. How on earth had she managed to break the silly thing off? She didn't think she'd pulled on the wrench that hard. Then, again, maybe she didn't know her own strength.

On the other hand, what else was new? Everything around here was either broken or rotting. Setting the corroded handle on the kitchen table, she glanced over at Molly, who sat skeptically eyeing the treasure.

"This isn't a very good surprise," she pouted, picking up the broken main handle.

"No, it's not, is it?" Lark sighed, and leaning back in her chair, she picked up the book on plumbing. Hopefully it would have some usable advice. The problem with these books seemed to be that the people who wrote them had never seen a remodeling challenge quite like hers. "How

about if we rent a movie tonight, because you helped find
the treasure?"

"Yea!" Molly pushed away from the table. "Can we go
on another treasure hunt?"

"We'll see," Lark commented absently. "Right now, why
don't you go hunt for AWOL. She's probably around here
somewhere. Why don't you look upstairs?"

"Okay."

Lark listened to her daughter's retreating feet pound up
the stairs as she searched her manual for tips on fixing a
broken water main. The pounding continued to grow louder
until Lark finally realized that it wasn't coming from Molly
any more. The pounding seemed to be coming from the
front of the house.

Pulling open the front door, Lark was amazed to find
Cole, madder than a half-naked, dripping-wet hen. AWOL
was with him, growling and tugging playfully at the towel he
had precariously fastened at his hips.

What on earth? She stood for just an instant and took in
the lather-filled hair and soap-slicked skin, as Cole wrestled with and shouted at the gamboling AWOL. It was a
sight she wouldn't soon be able to forget. His summer tan
still glowed a healthy bronze. And from what she could
see—which, thanks to AWOL, was almost everything—he
was in magnificent shape.

"Dammit," he shrieked at the dog and ripped the back of
his towel from her jaws. AWOL immediately stopped playing and sat at his feet.

Lark smiled at Cole's unconscious use of Ben's command for the dog to sit. "I suppose that for this visit, at
least, I should be thankful you decided not to come through
the wall." She held the door open wider so he could stomp
furiously into her living room.

"Don't get cute," he ordered, tossing his bubble-filled hair out of his face. "I'm not in the mood for your sassy little repartee."

"Oh?" Lark lifted a delicate eyebrow. "So, what exactly is it you are in the mood for?" she asked, and immediately wished she hadn't.

"A shower for starters," he bellowed. "What have you done with the water?"

"I turned it off."

"I can see that much." He blinked rapidly as another drizzle of lather found his eye. "Turn it back on."

"I will. As soon as I rig up a temporary handle for the water main...."

"As soon as you rig up...?" Cole held out a soggy lock of his hair. "I'm supposed to wait for you to replumb this place before I can finish my shower? Are you crazy?"

Lark could see the ominous thunderclouds building above his head and suddenly wished she'd thought to warn him that she was turning off the water. "Listen, Cole. If you would just relax, I can have the water back on in no time. I just have a little broken-valve problem."

"Ah, life at the booby hatch. It just doesn't get any better than this, does it?" he growled, his voice dripping with sarcasm. AWOL, tired of listening to their conversation, began tugging at Cole's towel again. "I hope you know... that school starts...in a little over a week...." he panted as the dog did her best to relieve him of his towel. "And I will expect ... stop it! ... to be able to take a shower by then.... Sit!"

Lark could see the tan line at Cole's hips and couldn't stop herself from admiring the way the smooth, milky texture of his skin blended into his tropical tan. As he spun around in circles, trying to get the dog to let go, she reflected back on her big redheaded barrel of a husband, Ben.

No, Ben had certainly never looked like that. He was more the Pillsbury-doughboy type, all sort of cuddly and cute. But Cole... now, here was a different story.

"Lark, call off your dog!"

"Will you behave?" she taunted. "And promise not to tear down any more of my wall?"

"No. But I will promise to sue you if you don't get my shower back on.... Sit!"

"Okay, okay." Lark snapped her fingers. "Dammit, AWOL!" AWOL dropped the towel and looked expectantly at Lark. "Ben taught her that," she told Cole when he stared incredulously at the dog. "My late husband."

"Oh."

"Listen, you're going to have to let me get to work, if I'm going to get the water back on. I promise to have your water fixed within an hour or so."

"Yeah, right," he said with derision as he readjusted his towel. "Just like you fix everything around here." As he leapt over the hole she'd carved into her floor and stomped toward her front door, he spun around and glared at her through narrowed eyes. "I insist that you hire a handyman to fix the problems around here. I want someone who will come in here and do the job right the first time."

Drawing in a deep breath Lark stared at Cole, outraged at his bossy attitude. "I will do no such thing."

"Yes, you will." His eyes glittered angrily.

"Or what? You'll punish me?" She was tired of being treated like some kind of silly little child.

"Don't give me any ideas." He turned and took a step toward her.

"You can't threaten me." Her voice was shaky and her breathing was shallow as she met the fire in his eyes with her own. What gall. Besides, hadn't he given her his thirty-day notice? He seemed to have forgotten that particular threat.

Maybe she should remind him. Then, again, maybe now was not the time, she thought as he took another step closer and she could see the wheels of conflict turning in his brain.

He flexed his hands, a tortured expression on his face, which she recognized but did not entirely understand. She only knew that if she was going to save her last shred of dignity with this man, she had to get him out of her house. Fast. Before she made a fool of herself again. Luckily, Cole beat her to the punch.

"This is not a threat, Lark. I mean it. No more electrical work. No more plumbing. Hire someone qualified before you get yourself or someone else killed." With that last edict he left, slamming the door behind him.

Lark reached up and wiped a stray tear from her cheek. Cole was right. That was how she had lost Ben. He was always scheming for a quicker money-making way to do everything, and it had finally caught up with him.

She listened as Cole stormed into his apartment. Well, she thought, looking around miserably at the dump she'd inherited, tomorrow was another day. Tomorrow, she would hire a handyman.

Randy howled as he got a look at Cole's hair, which was slicked back into a stiff, stubby little ponytail. "New do, man? Or do you have some fashion-model inclinations that I'm unaware of?" Following his friend into his kitchen, Randy spoke confidentially. "You know, I heard the wethead is dead. Again."

"Shut up," Cole groused and handed him a beer.

"Oh, c'mon, buddy. This isn't like you. Where's your sense of humor?" Randy ambled into Cole's living room and took a long pull on his frosty bottle of beer. He flopped into the recliner and studied his friend thoughtfully.

Cole lay down on the couch and stared at the ceiling. "It got sucked out the window the second her sofa arrived. That and my sanity." Although if he were honest with Randy, he'd have to admit she threatened his sanity on more than one level.

"It's that bad?"

"You try writing a complex textbook in the middle of a train wreck. I'm not kidding, man. She can make more noise than a lumber mill over there."

"Is that all that's bothering you?"

Cole pulled his eyes away from the plywood that still covered his living room window and glared grumpily at Randy. "That's enough, isn't it?"

"I guess so," Randy agreed doubtfully. "But if you ask me, she's distracting on her own. In case you hadn't noticed, she's pretty hot stuff. I know I wouldn't be able to think straight if I knew she was right next door."

"Humph," Cole snorted. "You wouldn't be able to think straight if you knew Miss Piggy was next door."

"Hey." Randy pretended to be wounded, then grinned. "We should double-date sometime. Lark and me, and you and..." Randy paused and frowned in mock seriousness. "Who are you dating these days, anyway?"

"No one special, not that it's any of your business," Cole retorted defensively.

Randy clucked his tongue in disgust. "Roughly translated, no one. Never fear..." He patted his hip pocket, where he kept his A-list black book. "The Rand Man's here. I'll get you fixed up."

"No, thanks." Cole hoped the irritation he felt didn't show in his voice. Something about Randy taking Lark on a date stuck in his craw. "I remember the last time you set me up on a blind date. I still have back problems."

"Yeah," Randy smiled fondly at the memory. "Was she in great shape or what?"

Cole shook his head. "Yes, but did she have to keep demonstrating it? I'd have been perfectly happy to take her word on the black-belt issue."

Randy laughed. "Aw, come on. You have to admit going one or two rounds with her beats sitting alone on a Saturday night."

"No. I don't."

"Well, don't worry. I have plenty more where she came from." He grabbed Cole by the arm and clapped him jovially on the back. "Come on, let's get out of here and play a little handball at the rec center. You can catch a shower there. We'll go on my motorcycle since your car is still in the shop." Standing, he reached over and hauled Cole to his feet, patting him fondly on his head. "With this new hairdo of yours, you won't even need a helmet."

Shouting with laughter, Randy pushed his friend out the door.

Chapter Five

"Mr. Beaumont?"

"Yup. I'm him. I prefer to be called Buford, though. That's what my mama named me."

"Oh. Well, of course, then...Buford." Lark held open her screen door to admit her first—and only—candidate for the handyman job.

Much to her extreme annoyance, she had to concede that Cole had a point about her needing help. Besides, this was good practice. She had to interview a day-care provider this afternoon for Molly. Might as well hone her hiring skills on this guy.

She watched in fascination as the leathery, old duffer shuffled slowly into her living room and settled comfortably into her lumpy easy chair. She'd scoured the paper and phone book all morning, looking for reliable help. Buford Beaumont had been the only person able or willing to come to her assistance.

Taking in the excruciatingly slow fashion in which he dug a match out of his pocket, struck it on his shoe and lit his corncob pipe, Lark was beginning to wonder just how able he was. He was certainly eighty, if he was a day.

"Well, little lady, just what is it you'll be needin'?" Buford's watery blue eyes traveled slowly around the room and down to the large gaping hole chopped in her living room floor. His eyes widened slightly.

"Actually, I..."

"Looks like you started without me," Buford interrupted. "Umm, umm, umm." He shook his head and puffed lazily on his pipe.

"Uh, yes. We have a bit of a dry rot probl—"

"What else you got torn apart around here?"

Lark shook her head slightly. He was obviously hard of hearing or he didn't give a rip about the answers to his questions.

"I started to install a new circuit panel, but..."

"What do you know about circuit panels, little lady?" Buford blew a hazy cloud around his head. "Seems to me you're anglin' to get yourself killed. Nope, no, nah. That's no good. Better leave them circuits to me."

Lark bristled at his chauvinistic attitude. Between this guy and Cole, she was beginning to feel like some kind of wilting debutante. None of the ranch hands had ever treated her this way. Still, he was all that was available in her price range. Maybe she should give him a chance despite his little idiosyncrasies.

Reaching up, he scratched the stubbly gray fringe that surrounded his balding pate. "What else needs doin'?"

"Well, we have some plumbing problems, and we have no water. I accidentally broke the handle off the water main when I..."

"Uh-oh. Nope, no, nah. Can't have that. Better get that fixed. Got somethin' out in the van that might getcha squared away. What else?" Buford stuffed his hands into the tightly stretched bib of his grease-and-paint spattered overalls, and squinted at her through the cloud of smoke his pipe was creating.

Lark sighed. "Mr. Beaumont..."

"Buford. It's what I answer to."

"Buford," she nodded impatiently. "There isn't much around here that doesn't need fixing. The roof has..."

"Okay."

"Okay what?"

"Okay, I'll take the job."

"You will?"

"Yep, yep, yep," he droned, puffing thoughtfully on his pipe. "But I'm gonna need some up-front money." He named a sum. "Figure I can get started on that."

Lark mentally calculated her meager savings and decided she could afford him. Barely. He seemed to know what he was talking about, at least as far as she could tell from her studies of the home-improvement books. Anyway, at this point she didn't have much choice.

Retrieving her checkbook from her purse, she wrote him a check for the amount he required and told him she would pay the rest on completion of the job.

"Okay." Buford ran a meaty hand over his sagging jowls. "I can be here Monday next."

"Monday next?" What was that? This coming Monday or next Monday? She didn't care. Just as long as he showed up.

"Yup. Gotta wrap up a little job I'm doing for my uncle down at his hardware store."

Uncle? Heavens. How old must *he* be? Lark held the check in her hand for a moment, wondering if she should be asking a few more questions before she handed over part of her precious nest egg. "Buford, where exactly are you from?"

"Originally?"

Lark nodded.

"Nawlins."

Nawlins? Must be some small town near by. The Midwest was filled with crazily named little communities. "Do you have family there?"

"Just my mama. My uncle, her brother, lives here in Springfield with me. Yep, yep, yep. I go visit Mama as often as possible. She's gettin' up there."

Lark could only imagine. Never having hired a handyman before, she guessed the interview process had concluded. She couldn't think of anything else she wanted or needed to know. Leaning over to Buford, she handed him the check.

"Thanks. I'll get the handle to your water main back on for ya today. Nope, no, nah. Can't go around with no water." Standing he shuffled slowly to the front door. "First off, though, I need some pie and coffee. Break time," he announced, and with that shuffled slowly out to his ancient-looking van.

Ladders and buckets of tools, ropes and cords of all sizes and supplies of every kind adorned the top and sides of the dented vehicle. Ever so slowly, he backed out the driveway into the street and crawled at a snail's pace toward the pie shop on the corner.

The following Monday, still unable to find his briefcase and several other teaching aids that had suddenly come up missing, Cole trotted into his first class of the semester. He was late and that made him cranky.

Luckily for Cole, Lark had finally gotten the water turned back on, so at least he'd been able to shower this morning. And in the past week he'd also made some kind of headway on his textbook...between the periods of pandemonium that filtered through the plywood Lark had nailed to cover the hole in their mutual wall. He hadn't laid eyes on her in days, but he could tell that she and Molly were alive and kicking by their clamor.

Funny thing was, he was almost getting used to it. He'd been able to concentrate through some of the most amazing racket and was nearly back to the point in his project at which Lark had turned off the electricity. This time, though, he'd played it smart and saved his work every step of the way.

Yanking off his backpack and tossing it on the table at the front of the classroom, he turned to survey this year's crop of students. Fresh young faces of every sort looked expectantly at him, waiting for him to fill their heads with useful information that they could take with them out to the real world, where they would...

His wandering gaze screeched to a sudden halt when it crashed into a pair of large violet eyes that stared back at him with equal shock and dismay.

Lark.

What the devil was she doing there? It was bad enough having to listen to her all day and night, but to have to look at her at work, too? He was most certainly going to lose his mind. Shaking his head in exasperation, he reached for his backpack and began passing out the syllabus for the term.

Cole was Professor Richardson? Oh, good Lord. How could she have been so blind? He wasn't some aging undergrad. He was her teacher. He held the power to destroy her grade-point average in the palm of his hand. No doubt he would flunk her out of spite.

Thank heavens nothing more had been said about her evicting him. He hadn't mentioned his thirty-day notice again either, which was a good sign. As long as he was her tenant, she felt she had some small amount of control over the situation. But then, she shifted uneasily in her seat, so did he now that she was his student. She stared down at the syllabus she held, cheeks burning, and surveyed with trepidation the list of test dates and selected readings for the course.

As she scanned the sheet she wondered if it was too late to transfer out of his class. No. She'd checked. This was the only beginning computer class offered this term, and she needed it for her major. She had been lucky to squeeze into this overly popular class as it was.

Lark watched Cole move between the rows of seats as he passed along another round of handouts and quickly averted her gaze when his eyes found and locked with hers.

Trying to make herself focus on the growing stack of information being passed her way, Lark felt herself begin to panic. What was she doing here? She was no student. What did she know about computers? As far as she knew she'd never even touched one before. And now here she was at the mercy of Professor Cole.

"Is he, like, totally gorgeous or what?"

"I'm in pain."

"He could, like, hurt you with those looks."

"Umm. Total pain. He's really cute for, like, you know, an older guy."

"I am in love with his hair. Could you just die? It's so thick and long and you know, goldish, sort of... I wonder if he has it streaked."

"Oh, get over it. He's, like, a man. Real men don't get their hair streaked. I personally love his smile. Totally painful. The bod is pretty killer, too."

"I can tell already I'm going to love this class."

The two freshmen seated behind Lark giggled.

If they only knew what a jerk he could be they'd change their tune, Lark thought sourly and tightly gripped the pages in her hand. He was a total pain all right. A pain in the . . .

Still, she had to admit, they had a point. Looking at him through their eyes, she could see a handsome, sexy, dynamic man who was obviously in his element as he addressed the class, introducing himself and the nature of the course. If she were ten years younger, she might be inclined to drift through his class, fantasizing about some romantic scenario where they were stranded together on a deserted tropical island.

But no. That's not why she was here. She was here to learn a skill, so that she could take care of her daughter and herself.

"Ms. St. Clair?"

Lark was mortified to feel the eyes of the entire class on her as Cole called her name. Gosh darn it anyway, she'd been caught woolgathering. What was the question? She searched in blind desperation for the threads of the discussion that had gone on without her and came up empty-handed.

"I'm sorry," she stammered, the caustic tone of his voice making her flush with shame.

"I asked you if you had any experience with DOS." He folded his arms across his chest, and legs spread slightly for balance, regarded her skeptically.

"Dos is good," she replied in a German accent, causing laughter to ripple through the crowd.

Cole rolled his eyes. "I'll take that as a no."

So she didn't know what DOS was. That was no reason to flunk her, was it? She was a quick study—she would just figure it out. Nervously, she nibbled on her pencil.

Moving along, Cole got a consensus for this class's particular experience with computers, and it seemed from all accounts that Lark was the only computer illiterate in the bunch.

The bell in the union clock tower signaled the end of class and Cole gathered the questionnaires he'd given to his students, reminding them to read chapter one in the assigned textbook before the next class. As the group filed quickly out the door, he was again struck by the beauty with the violet eyes. Much to his chagrin, he had to admit she was far and away the prettiest girl in class.

"I love you! You love me!"

Molly shouted along with the television for the millionth time as Lark sat on the couch trying to make sense of Cole's handouts. She'd have spread the information out on the kitchen table, but Buford had been there earlier in the day and it was covered with an odd assortment of his particular tools and gadgets. She was unable to tell what he'd been up to, but by the size of the holes in her walls it was enough.

As much as she enjoyed her daughter's creative music, Lark found she was unable to concentrate with all the racket. It gave her a sudden empathy for Cole's situation. She had to admit it must be hard to write with all the remodeling she'd been doing. She wondered about the nature of his book and if it was really as important as he seemed to feel it was.

"I love you! You love me!"

Maybe Cole wouldn't mind if she just slipped over there and asked him her questions in person. Worth a try, she decided, smiling as Molly danced across what was left of the living room floor.

"Molly, I'll be right next door for a few minutes. Keep the front door locked and don't let anyone in unless it's me, okay?" AWOL, obviously bored with the television show, trotted after Lark as she walked to the door.

"Okay!" she shouted in beat to the music.

"If you need anything, pound on the plywood—okay?"

"Okay!"

Cole pulled open his front door and was immediately annoyed at how happy he was to see Lark.

"Hi."

"Hi," she replied shyly. "I hope you're not in the middle of something important...."

Actually, he was very busy, the deadline for his textbook looming only three short months away. That and keeping up with his students kept him more than occupied.

"No, no," he hastily reassured her. "I was just, uh, writing."

"Oh." Her face fell slightly. "I can come back, this isn't important, really."

"No, come on in." He held the door open for her. She moved inside, and the dog, breathing heavily, came clicking in after her.

"I just had a couple of questions about the course and was trying to find the answers in your handouts, but with the TV and all..." She gestured to the wall, through which filtered strains of Molly's enthusiastic caterwauling. "I couldn't exactly concentrate."

Cole grinned. "I know the feeling."

"Sorry," Lark said sheepishly.

"She does love to sing, doesn't she?" Cole led her over to his sofa and gestured for her to sit down.

"Umm-hum. She gets it from her father. He loved to sing, too." She shook her head and grinned. "Couldn't carry a tune in a bucket." Settling down in her seat opposite Cole, she was suddenly shy.

"I...uh...just had a few questions about the course."

Cole leaned back in his chair and regarded her in amusement. "I read the questionnaire you filled out today." He cleared his throat and tried not to laugh. "I take it that the closest you've ever come to a computer is the U-bank machine at the Piggly-Wiggly in Butteville."

"Umm, actually, yes. But, I'm a quick learner," she hastened to assure him. "I'm sure I'll be able to keep up with the class just fine, as long as I know what the test will cover...." Her cheeks grew bright. "Not the exact information, of course, but, you know, how much is from textbooks and how much is from the lecture and...how much is from practical...experience."

Cole pulled a tennis shoe-clad foot up over his knee and watched her grow more flustered with each question. This was a side of her he'd never seen. Vulnerable. Worried. In a little bit over her head. She was beginning to seem almost human.

"So, what is it exactly, short of the test answers, that you want to know?" he teased.

"Well, for example, if I know the textbook from cover to cover, will I be able to pass?" Her gaze regarded him intently.

"Lark, I guarantee if you know the information in the textbook from cover to cover, you will pass. With flying colors."

"Really?" She seemed pleased.

"Really." He watched the pink stains of pleasure color the flawless skin of her cheeks and was taken back again by her incredible beauty. She could easily grace the most elite function in the highest of social circles, yet she'd married a rancher from Butteville. Why? he wondered. He was sure that like his ex-wife, Lark's looks could grant her every wish. So, what was she doing wasting her time on this dog of a duplex?

For the next thirty minutes, much to Cole's extreme surprise, he and Lark managed to have a civilized conversation. He was amazed. He hadn't thought it could be done. They laughed, they teased, they flirted shamelessly. He was impressed by her quick wit and her mind, and he could tell that she was impressed with him as a professor.

A small warning voice, deep in his subconscious, told him not to get too friendly with a student. That always spelled trouble. And trouble with women was something he avoided at all costs. Even though he sometimes got the feeling that this particular woman might be worth the trouble. He watched her run her fingers through her wild, silky mane and felt something involuntarily tighten in the pit of his stomach. She was so beautiful.

Luckily, the music from next door was coming to an end, signaling his sexy landlord that it was time to leave.

"Come on, AWOL." She snapped her fingers at the dog, who'd been content to root through Cole's laundry basket and chew on his underthings. "It's time to go." Tail wagging, the dog dropped Cole's socks and trotted to Lark's side. "Thanks," she said shyly, as she led the dog to the front door. "I appreciate your taking the time to answer my questions."

"My pleasure," he replied, unwilling to admit that those words were more than true. "Any time you need help on your homework, just hop on over."

"Maybe I'll do that," she smiled, training her irresistible eyes up at him and proceeding to draw him further into a web she had no idea she had even spun.

Chapter Six

"I have to go again?" Molly's face puckered into a worried frown.

"Yes," Lark assured her and began weaving an expert French braid into her daughter's hair. "Didn't you have fun yesterday?"

Molly shrugged noncommittally. "I guess so. Do I have to go every day?"

"Oh, no. Only on the days I have school. I thought you would be happy to have some other kids to play with."

"They're booboo heads."

"Booboo heads? Who's a booboo head?" Lark tugged on Molly's braid. Nobody was a booboo head to her daughter and lived to tell the tale.

"Donny. He's mean. He chases me and says he's going to kiss me." The child scrubbed her hands over her freckled cheeks in disgust.

"Oh, sweetheart, that's only because he likes you. Boys are like that. Sometimes they're mean to you because they

are trying to show you how much they like you." Images of
Cole bursting through her wall flitted through her mind.
"At least when they're little like Donny... Didn't you do
anything at day-care yesterday that was fun?"

"We sang," the child said, her eyes brightening. "And we
played with clay."

"Well, that's a pretty successful day in my book." Tying
a large green bow at the end of the satiny rust-colored braid,
Lark put the finishing touches on Molly's hair and lifted her
off the chair.

"Go grab your coat and hat. I don't want to be late for
my classes today," she told the child who quickly bounded
up the stairs to her room.

The day before had been Molly's first full day at day-care,
and Lark was having some separation anxiety herself.
Luckily, her daughter had taken an immediate liking to the
matronly Mrs. Spring, who ran a small day-care out of her
home just a few blocks away from the duplex. She came
with excellent references, and the tidy home smelled of
fresh-baked bread. Mrs. Spring watched six other children
approximately Molly's age, whose parents either worked
full-time or went to school. The best part was, Mrs. Spring
had no objection to watching the children at night for the
occasional evening class. She was affordable, and the loving older woman was the only thing that made being apart
from her daughter bearable.

Quickly tossing her textbooks and other necessary items
into her backpack, Lark called upstairs for Molly to hurry
as Buford arrived.

"You got a heap of plumbing problems, little lady," Buford began without preamble, bursting through the screen
door as if he owned the place. "But don't you worry none—
I can fix 'em. Already started, as you can see." He gestured
to the series of holes punched in the walls around the room.

Molly trotted down the stairs and stood behind her mother, gaping up at the old pipe-smoking duffer with interest.

"Well, I'm glad. It's nice to know . . ."

"Nothin' to be glad about, little lady," Buford broke in. "Plumbing is tricky stuff at best, and this here is far from the best."

"What I meant was . . ."

"Nope, no, nah. Never seen such a mess in all my born days. Not to worry, though. I'm gonna spend the whole day tearing out the old stuff in the apartment next door. That's the most important half of the building. This here is secondary stuff. I'll do this next." He pointed at her walls, explaining his convoluted and somewhat eccentric game plan as he went, his voice growing dim as he headed out into the hallway.

"I want to stay here and watch," Molly whispered.

Lark shook her head. "Goodbye, Buford," she called, as the man disappeared into the next room, seeming not to notice or care that she was no longer listening. Grasping Molly tightly by the hand, she said, "Come on, honey, we're late."

As the last of his upper-level computer-science class streamed out the classroom door, Cole stretched and glanced down at his watch. Nearly noon. It had been a long, exhausting morning, and he was hungry and tired. Keeping one step ahead of the bright minds of tomorrow was sometimes a daunting task.

Visions of Lark's pretty face drifted unexpectedly through his mind, exciting and rejuvenating him. Maybe, if he hurried, he could make it home for a leisurely lunch, catch a glimpse of his lovely landlord and make it back in time for his 2:30 lecture that afternoon. Maybe she would have some

more questions about his class. Lark's unexpected visit had
been a most pleasant surprise. He couldn't remember enjoying an evening so much in a long time. Not that he ever
took the time away from his writing or class work to just
enjoy life. It was a mode he'd gotten into years ago, after the
breakup of his marriage. A protective mode that had seen
him through the darkest period in his life. With the excep-
tion of an occasional boys' night out instigated by Randy,
Cole had pretty much operated in that singular mode for
years now.

But not today.

Grabbing his backpack, he loaded it with his paraphernalia and headed out to the faculty parking lot, where
with a roar of his newly repaired engine, he sped toward
home . . . and Lark.

The old clock tower chimed noon in the Memorial Union
quad. Looking at her afternoon schedule, Lark figured she
could save herself several dollars if she went home for lunch.
It probably wouldn't hurt to check on Buford either, she
mused as she started down the tree-lined street toward home.

Fall had definitely arrived. The smell of burning leaves
teased her nose, and the newly denuded tree branches
reached up to the sky for the last of the sun's warmth before winter set in. Lark loved this time of year. It reminded
her of plaid skirts, wool sweaters, bonfires and attending
football games as a high school freshman—Ben had been a
fullback his senior year.

He'd been such a mischievous boy, she remembered
fondly, shuffling along, enjoying the sun's slanting rays as
they bathed her face with their golden glow. Always a
schemer, trying to dream up a better, quicker way to make
a dollar. She'd fallen for his grand-scale plans to escape
from the small town that stifled him.

At eighteen she'd fancied herself in love and wanted to help him succeed with every fiber of her youthful heart. But real love was something more than a few stolen kisses under the bleachers after a football game, and as the years had gone by, there had been no helping Ben St. Clair. No saving him from himself. In the end it was one of his schemes that had gotten him killed and left his wife and young child in a state of financial ruin.

Lark knew she was finally beginning to come to the place where she could forgive Ben for losing everything and forgive herself for marrying the wrong man. But she knew it would still take more time and a lot of bitter tears before she completely healed.

Never again. She was an independent woman now. And she was going to stay that way. She had no time any more for men who chased pots of gold at the end of the rainbow. Not even handsome professors with fanciful dreams of writing the great American textbook.

What was it about Lark St. Clair that had him turning so eagerly down the street where they lived? Cole wondered, expertly threading his way through the multitude of bicyclists that crowded the college streets. Ever since she and her munchkin had moved in next door, he hadn't been able to think straight. He'd misplaced everything from his toothbrush to his briefcase while daydreaming about her, and that wasn't all. Many a night had been spent tossing and turning, wondering if she was safe and sleeping well. Wondering what she looked like in the moonlight, as it streamed in through the window to kiss her perfect cheeks. Wondering what it would be like to...

As Cole pulled the newly repaired Porsche up to the curb in front of his duplex apartment, he was stunned to see most of his furniture sitting outside on their lawn. What the hell?

One of the kookiest old men Cole had ever laid eyes on came staggering across his front porch in hip waders, carrying his computer and monitor, the keyboard dangling precariously from his arm. Dumping his load unceremoniously on Cole's kitchen table, now positioned among the scraggly rosebushes, the old coot headed back inside for another load.

Slamming on the brakes, Cole bounced up over the curb, screeched to a stop and leapt out of his car, impatiently pushing his long hair from his face as he flew to his front porch. If Cole was in the process of being burglarized, he was going to put a stop to it right now. Pulverizing the old guy would be no problem, but what about his accomplices? Maybe he should call for help.

No time. He was far too mad.

"Hey, now," Buford called from behind Cole's CD player and speakers, as he came out of the front door once more. "You don't want to be goin' in there. Leastwise not until I can turn off the 'lectricity. Nope," the old man informed him as he tripped down the stairs and stumbled past him toward the kitchen table. "Too damn much water. Could get yourself 'lectrocuted. Wouldn't want that now, wouldja?"

Still in shock, Cole stood and watched the old man drop his stereo equipment next to his computer. Too damn much water? What did that mean? Was this some kind of old-time burglar jargon? It wasn't until the steady flow at his feet started to seep through his shoes that Cole began to notice there was a fair amount of water running from under his front door and over his porch.

Fair amount, nothing—it was a damn waterfall. Stunned, Cole moved past the plywood that still covered his plate-glass window, across the porch to the window around the corner, only to discover that his apartment was flooded with about three feet of water. Water that seemed to be rising.

And flowing out from under the door... to the yard... to his furniture...

His computer. His priceless disks. His future.

Running frantically over to the kitchen table, Cole inspected the pile of electronics and office supplies that had been his textbook in the making and breathed somewhat easier. Everything seemed to be there. Satisfied that all was not lost, Cole turned and strode over to Buford who was now carrying his television to the table.

"Uh, excuse me." Cole tapped the old man on the shoulder as he pushed the TV in next to the stereo. "But would you mind telling me just exactly who you are?"

Buford turned around and extended a meaty hand. "Didn't the little missus tell ya? I'm your handyman. Buford Beaumont." He pumped Cole's hand for a moment, then dropped it to scratch the shiny bald spot at the top of his head. "I don't mind tellin' ya, this is the damnedest thing I've ever seen. Those rusty old pipes would have like to exploded. I'd have caught it sooner, but I was down at the café takin' a pie break. Anyway, came back and found a regular geyser in your place, just like Old Faithful. Thought I'd try to save some of your stuff here, before I shut off the main. Got that main rigged up so the little missus can't go turn it off when she gets a bee in her bonnet, so it'll take me a spell to get the flow stopped. Ya know, you're lucky...."

Buford droned on as Cole impatiently tapped his foot and waited for a break in the man's diatribe. Finally deciding it would never come, as Buford began describing the great flood of 1908—or was it 1909?—Cole jumped in.

"Uh, Buford, that's fascinating and all, but on a more urgent note, exactly when do you plan on draining the lake in my living room? And even more importantly, when can I move all my stuff back in? I have a textbook due in just three mo—"

"Oh, nope, no, nah. You can't move back in there. No sir. Not now, leastwise. But don't worry. I know what to do. Luckily for you, it's just on the one side of the duplex. So far, the other side is still as dry as a bone."

"Lucky for me," Cole echoed, as Buford went on about the horrific amount of work it would take to put Cole's plumbing back together. What the heck was he going to do now? Like Bethlehem at Christmastime, there wasn't another room—or manger—to be had in Springfield. "Lucky for me," he chanted and sank down in his easy chair—now positioned with the best possible view the yard had to offer—smack-dab in the middle of the sidewalk.

Lark rounded the corner of her street to find a group of people standing in her yard, milling around what looked like a yard sale. Cole was raking his hands through his hair, gesturing wildly to Buford, who stood placidly smoking his pipe and nodding thoughtfully.

As she picked up her pace and drew closer, she could hear Buford say, "Nah, probably won't have it completely drained till morning. By then it'll be safe for you to go back and get the rest of your stuff. But you won't be moving back in there for quite a spell. No sir. Near as I can figure, it will take several days for the place to dry out and then, of course, I'm going to have to rip out the rest of your pipes and replace a bunch of water-damaged flooring. Probably gonna cost the missus a little more than we figured. The pipes are shot. All of 'em. That'll take some time. You won't be back in there for a while."

As if he felt Lark's arrival, Cole turned and shot her a wild look.

"What's happening?" she ventured timidly, not liking the look of the scene unfolding before her.

"What's happening? I'll tell you what's happening," Cole moaned in agitation. "This *handyman* you hired," he gestured wildly at Buford's back as he retreated into his apartment, "has flooded me out of house and home. What the devil am I supposed to do now? There is a housing crisis in this town, for crying in the night. I should know. When you first moved in, I tried to find a room. Even in a crummy motel, and they were all rented to students on waiting lists for dorm rooms and apartments. There is no place for me to go."

Raking his hands over his face, he lifted his eyes to scan the sky for signs of rain. "How the hell am I supposed to write a textbook out here on the damn lawn?"

Lark watched helplessly as Cole walked over to his bed—so thoughtfully set up under a tree—and flopped down on it, covering his face with his hands.

She felt terrible. This was all her fault, she thought, fighting the waves of anxiety that knotted inside her. Every time she turned around, this remodeling situation just seemed to get worse.

Maybe she should just cut her losses and sell the darn thing. But, then, who in his right mind would buy a broken-down half-torn-apart flooded-out duplex? She tried to envision that ad in her mind.

This lovely duplex sits in a lush natural setting. A little tender loving care will bring this classic back to its original splendor. Air-conditioned by nature's breezes, this home sports its own indoor swimming pool....

Biting her tongue, she battled a wave of hysterical laughter that bubbled up in her throat. Cole looked so miserable and dejected, the hysterical laughter suddenly turned to just plain hysteria.

Even though she had her doubts about the mass-market appeal of a book on some sort of computer gadget, she knew how much it meant to Cole. And now—no thanks to her and her bumbling handyman—he was homeless. She knew he'd worked like a dog on this book. Much harder than Ben had ever worked on one of his wild schemes. She also knew that he was nearly done and that his deadline at the university press couldn't be far off.

With a great deal of fear and reluctance, Lark approached his bed and perched timidly on the edge. If it weren't for Molly, she'd offer to camp out in the yard and let him take her place. But she had a daughter to think about.

A rather crazy idea began to form in her mind as Buford approached. No, she thought, he would probably never go for it. But then, again, maybe in some small way she could make all this up to him....

Her thoughts were interrupted by Buford's return. "Ya'll won't have any water for a while," the handyman warned them. "The water's off at the main."

Cole peered between his fingers and stared at the old man through narrowed eyes. "Lack of water doesn't seem to be a problem at the moment," he snapped irritably.

People walked and cycled past on the street, looking curiously at the odd scene in Lark's yard, but she didn't care. All she could see at the moment was Cole and his dream being washed away in a sea of rusty water.

Buford seemed not to notice or care about Cole's discomfiture. "Don't worry though. I can rig it up today so that the other side has water before I go home. First off, though, I'm going to take a break. Back soon," he informed them, climbing into his van and backing at a turtle's pace into the street.

Lark watched him drive away and knew that they only had one recourse. "Uh, Cole?"

"What now?" he groaned, rolling over on the mattress to face her.

He looked so boyish and vulnerable lying there, Lark longed to reach out, smooth his hair away from his brow and ease the lines of worry that had formed there. Instead, she reached out and touched him sympathetically on his arm and felt her heart begin to melt.

"I was just thinking..."

Cole pushed himself up to a sitting position and swung around next to her, his thigh lightly brushing hers. "Do me a favor," he ordered. "Don't think."

"But this is a good idea."

"I've heard about as many of your good ideas as I can take." He shot her a baleful look.

"No, really."

"Okay." He sighed, shrugging hopelessly. "Hit me."

"Well," she began, suddenly shy. Suddenly fearful of his rejection. "I was just thinking that you should move in with me."

Cole's laughter was sharp. "Are you kidding?"

"No," she said defensively. "What else are you going to do?"

"I don't know yet. I need to give it some thought. But I know the answer isn't moving in with you. I'd lose my mind."

Lark did her best to ignore his hurtful words. "Listen. You have nowhere else to go—you said so yourself. Last night you told me that you have to lecture all afternoon today. What are you going to do with all your stuff? Leave it out here in the yard unattended? I guarantee it won't be here when you get back. Plus..." she looked up at the darkening sky "...I wouldn't count on the weather holding."

She watched as he darted a worried look at the clouds that were rolling in. Figuring she had him on the line, she went in for the kill. "You can't stay in your place for a few days, and Buford will be there making all kinds of racket anyway. Why don't you move in with us, where it's dry and quiet."

Cole raised a skeptical eyebrow.

"Honest. We'll be quiet as church mice. You won't even know we're there."

Still silent, Cole leaned back on the bed and pondered her words.

"We can store most of your stuff on my back porch," she continued arguing her point, "and the things you need, we can put in Molly's room. She can bunk with me for a while." Lark shrugged and stood up to leave. "Why don't you think about it."

Cole watched her walk across the yard, up the stairs to his side of the porch and peer in the side window at his water-logged apartment. He had to admit her arguments were sound. But that wasn't the point. Deep down inside, he knew that moving in with Lark would be a mistake on more than one level. He was already incredibly attracted to her. There was no way on earth he would ever be able to concentrate on his book if they lived together. It was almost more than his poor libido could stand.

Laying in bed night after night on his side of the duplex dreaming of Lark was bad enough. But knowing that she was merely across the hall... He was only human. How much could a man be expected to take? He'd been out of the social scene for far too long, and until recently that was the way he had liked it. Whether she knew it or not, Lark St. Clair had turned his entire neatly ordered academic world on its ear.

Then again, he mused, what other options did he have? She was right. He had nowhere else to go. It was going to start raining any minute now, and in just over an hour he had to be on campus lecturing a group of postgrad students.

Suddenly coming to a decision, he leapt to his feet and shouted across the yard—much to the amusement of a crowd of garage-sale groupies who were busily inspecting his possessions for purchase—"Okay. I'll move in with you. Are you happy now?"

Her answering smile stole his breath away, serving only to further convince him that he was definitely making the mistake of his life.

Chapter Seven

"If we put your easy chair on top of your sofa, we should have room for your bed and dresser," Lark said, eyeing what was left of the space on her back porch. "We'll cover it all with plastic. Then everything will be safe and dry under here. And that pile in the living room ... We can bring all that up to Molly's room tonight after class, when we move her in with me."

"Sounds like a plan. I'll do it though. You'd better get going or you'll be late for your class." Cole followed her through her apartment back outside to the front yard where only two remaining pieces of furniture waited to be rescued. They'd worked like dogs for the past hour, pulling almost everything he owned to the safety of her back porch, and once again Cole was amazed by her strength.

Lark shook her head. "No. I got you into this mess and I'll help get you out." She walked over and tentatively lifted her end of the bed.

"Okay, then. But you have to let me drive you to school as soon as we're finished."

Lark looked over at the shiny red Porsche Cole had parked so strategically over the curb and smiled. "Deal." Pushing a stray lock of hair out of her eyes, she sucked in a lungful of air and lifted the mattress high at his command.

"Have you eaten lunch yet?" he grunted, grappling his end of the bed up the porch stairs.

"No."

"We still have about twenty minutes before we have to be in class. Why don't I stop at the deli and get us a couple of sandwiches to eat on the way?"

Lark peeked out from behind her end of the mattress and grinned. "Okay."

So far, Cole mused, as they stuffed his mattress in with the rest of his furniture, living together wasn't bad. She was already much easier to work with than his ex-wife had ever been. Sherry would have sat on the porch complaining about her ruined manicure while she urged him to hurry and move everything by himself.

At least Lark was a good sport, he thought, as he watched her lift the heavy cascade of midnight hair from her shoulders and fan her delectable neck with her hand. And she was pretty easy on the eyes for a furniture mover, too.

Following her back out to the front yard, he battled the urge to shadowbox the rosebushes and work off some of the sexual tension that coiled inside him at the thought of living with this woman. No. He couldn't beat up the side of the house now. She'd think he was nuts. Come to think of it, he decided, as he watched Lark's hips sway down the front steps, he was nuts.

Buford arrived just as they'd finished up.

"You kids go on with you now," he instructed, dragging a large, unwieldy contraption from the back of his van.

"I'm just gonna start pumpin' the water out of the other side. Should be dry as a bone by tomorrow mornin'. Then I'll get on those pipes. Don't worry none about me now, I know what I'm doin'...."

Cole rolled his eyes at Lark as the old man slowly made his way toward the house, chattering a mile a minute to no one in particular.

"Come on," he whispered conspiratorially. "Let's get out of here before he decides it's time for another break." The sound of her tinkling laugh was revitalizing as he tucked her into the car beside him and headed toward campus.

"You what?" Randy, who'd been leaning back on the hind two legs of his chair, fell forward with a thud and stared in shock at his best friend.

"I moved in with Lark this afternoon."

Randy grinned devilishly. "Why you old son of a gun!"

Cole shook his head and stacked the papers he'd been grading into a neat pile on his desk in the office he kept at the computer-science department. Randy had a one-track mind. It was amazing that he had the fantastic reputation he did as one of the country's leading mathematicians, considering his every waking thought was of women.

He was fond of bragging that it was his head for figures that kept him so busy. And as corny as many of his buddy's lines were, Cole had to admit Randy never lacked for female companionship. Not that Cole envied his friend. The vapid, money-hungry women Randy went for usually turned Cole off.

Tapping his pencil on his desk top, Cole eyed his curious friend. "It's not what you think."

"Oh?" Randy propped his elbows on Cole's desk. "And just what is it I think?"

Cole smirked. "That we are having some kind of torrid affair."

Randy shook his head innocently. "Did I say that?"

"You didn't have to. It's written all over your lecherous face."

"So, you're not having a torrid affair?" Randy tented his fingers thoughtfully under his chin.

"Sorry to disappoint you, but no."

"Oh, I'm far from disappointed. Actually, this is great news."

Cole was puzzled. "What are you talking about?"

"Hey, buddy, if you don't want her, I'll be happy to step up to the plate. She's hot stuff."

"Back off, Kingman."

Randy shook his head in confusion. "But I thought you said . . ."

"I know what I said." What had he said? He wasn't sure why he was warning Randy away from Lark.

"So you do want her." Randy looked as if he found this piece of information particularly fascinating. "That's going to be tough."

Growing weary of his friend's tiresome conversation, Cole began to stuff his backpack with work he could do at home. Lark's home, he amended to himself, as a steel vise clamped down on his stomach. "What's going to be tough?" he asked, exasperated.

"Living platonically with that babe. How the hell are you ever going to get your book done?"

Cole shrugged. He found the less he thought about it, the less he had to worry about his book. "Most of the technical stuff is done and stored on disk. I just need to polish the prose and smooth out the rough edges. I have till the first of the year. Once I get back into my place, it should all pretty much fall together."

Cole zipped his pack closed and mentally crossed his fingers. At least he hoped that's the way it would work. He didn't really have much choice. There was no way he could finish the book over at her place. But if he played his cards right and burned a lot of midnight oil, he could finish in a couple of weeks. Provided, of course, that one raven-haired beauty could stay out of his consciousness for more than a few minutes at a time.

"Well." Randy hopped to his feet as Cole turned out the lights. "Good luck." He laughed, as though he knew a secret.

Ignoring him, Cole herded his buddy out the door and locked it behind them.

"Spin me again!" Molly screamed at Cole, staggering dizzily across the kitchen floor and back into his arms.

The sound of her delighted giggle filled the house, bringing a smile of joy to Lark's lips. Ben had never had much time to spend playing with his daughter, and Lark knew the child hungered for fatherly attention.

As she stood at the sink, cleaning and chopping vegetables for their dinner, Cole pushed the kitchen table up against the wall and reached for Molly.

"Okay, squirt. This time, you're an airplane." Bending low, he gripped one ankle and one arm, and lifting her into the air, spun her in circles. Cole imitated the sounds of a sputtering airplane as Molly shrieked with glee.

"Oh, no," Molly howled as her foot caught a basket that was hanging on the wall and sent it flying.

"Oops," Cole said sheepishly, and flew her down to the ground where she landed in a fit of giggles. "You're not a very good pilot, crashing into the wall like that. Where'd you learn to fly, anyway?"

"You!" she shouted. "Horse-ride me into the living room," she commanded, stumbling unsteadily to her feet and grabbing him around the leg.

"Molly, why don't you give Mr. Richardson a break?" Lark looked down at the pink-cheeked child before darting a glance at the pink-cheeked professor.

Still giggling so hard she could hardly speak, Molly looked up at her mother. "Why?"

"Because maybe he wants to rest—that's why."

The child looked up at Cole. "Do you want to rest?"

"I ain't dead yet, pardner. Let's ride," he shouted, and scooping her up onto his broad back he bolted out of the kitchen where he galloped around the hole in the living room floor.

Lark listened with pleasure to the sounds that reached her from the next room. Molly was thrilled at the prospect of having Cole stay with them and loved the idea that she would be bunking in with her mother. The whole ordeal took on the feel of a party in the child's mind. And as much as Lark hated to admit it, she was almost as excited as her daughter about having Cole stay with them.

It was wonderful to have a man around the house. Especially a man like Cole. Knowing that it was only for a few days also made it easier to reconcile her growing attraction to him. Soon he would be back on his side of the wall and she would stay on hers, and life as they knew it would go on.

Too bad though, she mused, listening to Molly shout giddyyap at their handsome tenant. He would make a natural father. She wondered absently why he'd never married and had children.

As Cole came charging through the kitchen again, he snatched another basket off the wall and popped it on Molly's head. "There's your cowboy hat, pardner. And here's your cigar," he announced, reaching around Lark's waist he snitched a carrot stick out of the pile she was cutting and stuck it in the child's open mouth.

"Okay, pardner," Molly screamed at an ear-splitting decibel level. "Let's ride!"

"Hey, hey, hey," Lark protested, flustered as Cole snaked his arm back around her body for a cigar of his own. "What do you think you're doing, Mr. Ed?" she joked and slapped his hand, hoping he couldn't see the effect his close proximity was having on her.

Cole patted her on the hip as he drew his hand from the vegetable bowl. "Haven't you ever heard of a carrot-smoking horse?"

"You're also a very friendly horse," she teased, removing the hand that rested so innocently on her hip.

Wiggling his eyebrows up and down, he said, "We aim to please."

"Why don't you aim toward the bathroom and wash up? Dinner's almost ready."

"Awww," Molly moaned, far from ready to settle down and eat.

Cole leaned back and looked into her freckled face. "She's kind of a party pooper, isn't she?"

"Yes," she pouted.

Pulling her mop of curls down close to his mouth, he whispered something in her ear that Lark couldn't hear. Molly giggled and held his head so that she could answer in kind. They whispered and laughed for a while, before Cole set her daughter on the ground and pointed her toward the bathroom. Together, they could be heard washing up and conspiring to do heaven only knew what during dinner.

Lark smiled. It was obvious that Molly adored Cole. It was also obvious that the feeling was mutual.

"That," Cole sighed contentedly, "was wonderful." Leaning back in his chair, he grinned at Molly. "Your mama is a terrific cook."

Molly nodded, her mouth full of fried chicken.

"Thanks, you two." Lark smiled and glanced at Cole. "I hope you saved some room for a piece of pie."

"Oh, I always have room for dessert." AWOL whined and scratched at the back door. "I'll get her," Cole offered, as Lark began to stack their dishes. "So, madam," he addressed the dog as she trotted to the edge of the table and looked appealingly at Lark for leftovers. "Just where have you been?"

"She disappears for days at a time. She always has. That's where she got her name," Lark informed him.

"Ah. So, you're always absent without leave?" Cole scratched the top of her head. "Is it just me, or are you getting kind of fat?"

Lark set a bowl of scrapings from their plates on the floor, which AWOL inhaled as if she were a canine vacuum cleaner. "She probably has gained a little weight since we've been here. She's used to having miles to run out on the ranch. It's a little cramped for a dog her size here in town. I think she wanders off more than usual here, too. She's bored."

"So, tell me..." Cole looked from the dog up to her master "...what was it like, living on a ranch?"

Lark shrugged as she moved to the counter, where she poured them each a cup of coffee and cut slices of freshly baked peach pie. "It had its good points," she said, and setting his coffee and pie in front of him, sat back down at the table. "I grew up in Butteville with Ben, Molly's father."

Sensing a boring adult conversation in the offing, Molly asked to be excused.

"Sure, honey. You can watch one video, and then it's time for bed."

Turning to Cole the wild-haired moppet asked, "Then will you tuck me in and tell me a story?"

Cole looked at Lark for permission. At her nod of approval, he ruffled the child's hair. "Sure, kiddo." Happy with that, Molly scampered off to sing along with the television.

"So, when you're done with your schooling, will you be moving back to the ranch?"

"Oh, no," Lark sighed, stirring some sugar into her coffee. "We had to sell it after my husband died. There were some financial problems.... Ben was not the best money manager there ever was. Funny thing about it is, I'm great with numbers. I want to be an accountant. But for his own reasons, Ben never trusted me with our books. I found out why after he died."

"Oh?" Cole lifted a curious eyebrow. He didn't push, but Lark could tell he was interested.

She smiled wanly. "Ben was sort of a rainbow chaser. Never content to just enjoy life. To just enjoy the blessings he had. His daughter, his ranch, his health ..."

"His wife," Cole supplied.

"That, too," she said, taking a sip of her coffee. "Anyway, I found out after he died that he'd invested in several sketchy get-rich-quick schemes, and it was one of those that finally led to his death."

Cole shook his head sympathetically but remained silent, allowing her to reminisce.

"It seems he bought into a gold mine somewhere in South Dakota. He didn't know it at the time, but the well was empty, so to speak. There wasn't a drop of gold in that shaft, other than the fillings in Ben's head and the ring on his finger."

"What happened?"

"It collapsed while he was exploring. By the time a rescue team got there to pull him out, it was too late."

"I'm sorry." Cole reached out and covered her hand with his.

"Me, too." Lark smiled at him and squeezed his thumb with her own. "Anyway, by the time I got his financial situation straightened out, all that was left was this duplex and a few dollars to go to school and learn a skill. I had no idea that this place was in such bad shape," she assured him. "If I had known, I'd have had Ben do something."

"Why do you suppose he let it fall apart this way?"

"Ben was always too busy pursuing the next dream to take care of the ones he already had. He went to school at Rand, you know. Bought this place to live in and rent while he was here and after he left he had no use for it any more, other than the income it generated every month. I guess he just couldn't be bothered. But, then, Ben could be that way about a lot of things...." Her eyes drifted toward the living room, where Molly could be heard singing about her love.

Cole's heart went out to Lark. He knew how it felt to be emotionally abandoned by the one you loved. Or at least thought you loved. She hadn't pulled her hand out from under his, and the warmth their hands generated began to thaw something deep in his soul.

"What about you?"

"What about me, what?" Cole hedged. He wasn't inclined to reveal much about his past to anyone. Especially old wounds left by Sherry. The fact that it had happened almost a lifetime ago made it seem even less real in his mind. How did one go about explaining that the last time he'd laid eyes on his son, Jake had been an infant? How would that sit with someone such as Lark, who would do anything for her child? Not very well, he was sure. No. He'd been young and foolish for relinquishing all rights to his son, and he understood that now. But would she? He might eventually tell her, but not tonight. Not after hearing that Ben was a less than ideal father. While they were getting to know each other, at least, he felt that they should keep things light. Besides, chances were this little infatuation would never go anywhere.

"Tell me about you," she urged.

"Not much to tell, really," he smiled up at her. "I fell in love with computers in high school and always had a knack for that type of thing."

"Funny."

"What's funny?"

"You don't look like one of those computer nerds, you know the kind with the pocket protectors and the tape around the broken horn-rimmed glasses."

Cole smiled. For some reason, he was thrilled that she didn't view him in that stereotypical way. "Thanks, I think."

"No," she mused. "You looked more like a beach bum."

Laughing, Cole squeezed her hand. "Thanks, I think."

Steering the conversation skillfully away from himself, Cole managed to find out a good deal more about Lark's plans for the future, the duplex and Molly. When those topics had been exhausted, they switched to the arts, sports, hobbies and music—both of whom agreed that the song now playing on the VCR was low on their top-40 list of favorites. And finally, much to their relief, the tape in question ended sending Molly back into the kitchen to say goodnight.

After Molly had been scrubbed, changed into pajamas, popped into bed and read to, Lark showed Cole to his new quarters.

"Hope you don't mind mermaid sheets." She grinned up at him as he stood in the doorway, dubiously eyeing the short twin bed.

"Sounds like a dream come true," he joked, glad actually that he wasn't sleeping out on the lawn.

"There are fresh towels in the linen cabinet next to the bathroom, and soap and shampoo and such are all sitting in the shower. Unless of course you have your own brands..."

She looked suddenly flustered at the mention of his personal effects.

"You know where the fridge is," she continued, "so make yourself at home if you get hungry or whatever."

"Thanks, I will," he said, grinning as she fussed unnecessarily over his mermaid pillows and blankets. Straightening up, she moved awkwardly over to the doorway and waited for him to come inside so she could pass.

They moved around each other like two gunfighters with itchy trigger fingers, wondering who would be the first to draw. As he circled the room, Cole stopped and turned to find Lark now leaning against the doorjamb.

"What's so funny?" he asked, his stomach jumping at her dazzling smile.

"You. In this room."

He grinned. "Yeah, well it beats the front yard." He took a step toward her. "Thanks." He took another step and squeezed her arm. "I don't know what I'd do without you."

Her bubbly laughter shone in her violet eyes. "Well, for starters, you'd probably be high and dry in your own place."

"True," he agreed, unable to resist the urge to run his hand up her arm to her jaw and trace the dimple that framed her cheek with his fingers. Time to say good-night, he decided, before he said or did something he'd regret. Just a friendly little hug by way of showing his thanks for all her help today, and then off to dreamland.

"Thanks for all your help today," he murmured as he drew her into his arms. Okay, that's enough, he told himself. Time to let go now, old boy. Just let go, Cole, he commanded as he tightened his arms, bringing her soft, pliant body more firmly into his embrace. Whatever you do, don't smell her hair, he thought, as he deeply inhaled the sweet floral scent that was uniquely Lark. Rocking her back and forth slightly he sighed and told himself that there was no way in hell that he was going to kiss her...as his lips sought and found hers.

No. No... He struggled for his sanity as she parted her lips and allowed him entrance to her mouth. She tasted so sweet and warm and feminine. His stomach churned and tightened as she sagged against the doorjamb, and gripping the cotton of his T-shirt, pulled him against her. Breathing raggedly, he kissed her, ignoring the warnings, savoring the moment.

Their kiss had a dreamy intimate quality that slowly silenced the voices in Cole's head and tried to persuade him there was room for two on the single bed behind them. He drew her into the room, deepening their kiss with a frenzied purpose that would have stunned him if he hadn't been so intent on his mission. As he reached for the top button of her blouse, Lark was the first to come to her senses.

Panting, she reached for and stilled his hand.

"I'm sorry," he breathed, cradling her head in his hands and trying to bring himself under control. "I didn't mean for that to happen."

"It's okay." Lark's reply was in a voice nearly as thready as his. "It's been kind of a crazy day." She lifted her large, darkly lashed eyes up to his, as if searching for what had motivated his kiss.

Cole smiled softly, knowing his emotions were written all over his face and not caring.

"Good night," he whispered, nudging her through the door while the voices in his head were once again strong enough to save them both.

"Good night," she murmured, slipping from the room. With one last, sweet, heart-stopping smile, she disappeared behind her door.

"Yep," he groaned, shutting Molly's door and sagging onto her tiny mattress, "you're in a heap of trouble, boy."

When—in the wee hours of the morning—Cole was finally able to drift off to sleep, would forever remain a mystery. For reasons he couldn't get a handle on, sleep had eluded him, driving him half out of his mind. Perhaps it was the five-foot-long mattress he'd had to coil his broad, lanky frame onto. Or perhaps it was the alluring beauty who slept peacefully just across the hall.

In any event, he'd been unable to keep his mind on the sheep that needed counting. At some point during the night, he'd come to terms with the fact that Lark was not his ex-wife and that it was unfair for him to treat her as such. He knew that he had to stop being so suspicious of all women, and eventually trust again. It would be hard, he knew, but Lark seemed like the kind of person anybody could trust.

Could he trust himself? That was the question. Reliving that insatiable kiss they'd shared just before bed was the real reason he had lain awake most of the night.

Cole groaned and rolled over on his side, attempting to pull his tangled feet out of Molly's little iron footboard as he went. The sun's soft fall rays began to filter into the room, bringing him out of his fitful state of slumber.

Opening his eyes to a painful squint, he was amused to find Molly leaning on her elbows at the edge of his bed, staring intently into his face. She grinned as he discovered her, and before she could react he reached out and grabbed her arm, tickling her as she screamed with laughter. She tickled him back and he pretended to collapse into fits of hysteria. In her childish way she amused him by showing him her favorite toys, singing a song or two and telling him about the time she'd tried to saddle and ride AWOL.

Finally, he sent her downstairs to fetch him a glass of orange juice so that he could get out of bed and run to the bathroom for a shower. Staggering out of the iron torture chamber, he stepped into the hallway only to collide with Lark as she emerged from the bathroom.

"Oh, I'm sorry," he muttered, trying not to stare at the skimpy nightgown that barely covered her long, lean thighs. Oh, yes. They were even better than he'd fantasized. The nightgown left little to the imagination, and with an effort worthy of a saint he was able to force his eyes up to her face. There he found her busy studying his bare torso. Planting his hands on his pajama-clad hips, he grinned. "Good morning."

"Ah...good morning," she squeaked, flustered. "Would you... uh...like some breakfast?" She seemed unable to meet his gaze.

"That would be great."

"Good. Okay. All right, then. I'll...just go make us some."

With that, she backed into her bedroom—smiling all the while—groped clumsily for the bathrobe that hung behind her door, then scooted past him and down the stairs.

"I don't suppose you've seen a file marked 'Handouts C.S. 101' laying around here somewhere have you?" Cole asked over a mouthful of Lark's delicious pancakes.

Lark's expression grew thoughtful as she blew on her coffee. "No...I don't think so. Where did you see it last?"

"I thought I set it in the living room yesterday when we were moving. I looked in there and all through Molly's room, and I can't find it anywhere."

"Do you need it right now?" she asked, looking worried.

"It would be handy. It's not the end of the world, but it just bugs me that I can't seem to hang on to anything."

"I'm sorry." Her eyes darted around the messy apartment in agitation.

"It's not your fault, I guess I'm just a little absentminded these days." Actually, it *was* all her fault, but he couldn't exactly tell her that it was her spunky little personality, her strength of character and the fabulous little package it all came wrapped in that was causing him to lose his organizational grip.

Lark's mouth curved in amusement at his choice of words. "Well, that sounds pretty normal for a professor."

"No pun intended?" He grinned.

"Of course." She returned his grin. "When Molly comes downstairs, we'll ask her if she's seen it. And I'll be sure to keep an eye out for it, too. I'm sure it will turn up somewhere."

"Can't finish today," Buford calmly told Lark that afternoon, a coil of pungent pipe smoke curling out of the corner of his mouth. The portly old man sat placidly on the floor in Cole's apartment, surrounded by great piles of rusty pipes that he'd scattered. Once again Lark had come home for lunch to check on Buford, hoping to spur him into action. So far, all he'd managed to accomplish in the half hour that she'd been there was a fairly vigorous workout of his jaw. The man sure could talk.

"Why not?" Cole's voice came from over Lark's shoulder, causing a warm flush of pleasure to stain her cheeks. Cole had come home for lunch. She was thrilled at the unexpected surprise. For moral support, she told herself.

"Well..." Buford puffed thoughtfully on his pipe. "For one thing, no nipples. Only have two. Need three for this job."

Cole shot Lark an incredulous look. *No nipples?* They gaped at each other in amazement. Lark felt as if they could read each other's minds. *What the devil is he talking about?* they wondered, staring at each other and then the old man.

"Nope, no, nah. Can't finish without enough nipples. Thought I'd go pick up some down at my uncle's hardware store, after I take a break." Hoisting himself up to his feet amid a deafening artillery spray of bone-popping noises, Buford staggered past them, slowly reaching a standing position as he headed toward his van. As he crawled out of the driveway, Cole looked down at Lark.

"No nipples?"

"Sounds like a personal problem." She grinned, and led him back to her place for lunch.

"Oh, for pity's sake," Lark exclaimed as she came back into the kitchen that evening.

"What is it?" Cole stopped bouncing Molly on his knee and turned his attention to her agitated mother.

She tossed him the note, tears burning in her eyes. "Here, I found this on the living room floor slipped under the door. You read it."

Sensing the serious nature of the missive, Cole let Molly slide to the floor as he stood up, unfolded the crumpled note, and read the shaky handwriting scratched there.

Ms. St. Clair:
I regret that due to circumstances beyond my control,
I must rush back to my hometown to visit my mama. I
will return as soon as I am able, and finish up your job.
                                Respectfully yours,
                                Buford Beaumont

Cole rolled his eyes and shook his head. Life was so nutty
right now, these little curveballs barely fazed him.

"What kind of work ethic is that?" Lark ranted, punching and rolling what was supposed to have been their meatloaf.

Cole clasped his hands over hers while there was still a
chance for the poor mound of beef. "Hey, now. Just calm
down. We'll think of something. We're all right," he said
soothingly, and moving behind her he began to rub the tense
muscles at the back of her neck.

Spanking the meatloaf with a resounding slap, Lark
turned in his arms to face him, furious purple darts shoot-
ing from her eyes. "How dare he take my money and run off
to visit his mama. We're desperate here! You know, I have
half a mind to climb into the truck and drive to Nawlins and
get that old coot."

"Good luck." Cole sighed, pulling her red and angry face
up against his chest. "Because New Orleans is a hell of a
long drive from Springfield, Kansas."

Chapter Eight

"Hold the light just a little higher," Cole grunted, as he lay on his back under the sink and peered up inside the wall. "That's good. Right there... No, you have to come closer, more toward me," he instructed hollowly from the inside of the cramped cabinet. "And point it up."

"I am!" Lark, who was struggling to point the flashlight to where she thought Cole was looking, ducked her head down inside along with his.

Straining to see in the shadowy light, Cole finally lost his patience. "Oh, for... Here..." Gripping Lark under her arms, he hauled her unceremoniously across his chest and guided her arm to the spot he was indicating.

"There. Much better," he praised, and Lark had to wonder if he was referring to the light or to the intimate nature of their position.

She didn't know about him, but she was definitely beginning to sweat. Her heart beat irregularly against his as she lay sprawled across his muscular frame. Funny, she'd never thought of plumbing as a contact sport before now.

"Yes..." His warm breath fanned the curls at her ear, tickling her. "This is much, much better."

"Better for whom?" Lark snapped, sliding slightly off to one side of Cole's body, as he adjusted something or another in the wall.

"Shh," he cautioned, slapping the wrench into her hand. "Don't mess with my concentration."

Lark snorted and tossed the wrench out onto his kitchen floor. Suddenly he was Mr. Fix-it.

Lifting his bottom slightly, he dragged the book on plumbing out from under him and propped it on Lark's head. "Hmm, Buford was right."

Craning her neck around the edge of the cover, Lark attempted to see what he found so fascinating in a book she'd read at least a dozen times. "Right about what?"

"We need nipples."

"What? No way. Let me see. I don't remember reading that. Is there some kind of centerfold in that thing that I missed?" Laughing, she grabbed for the book.

Batting her hand away, Cole held the book up under the flashlight for her inspection. "See, it says so right here in the section on plumbing parts."

"Well, I'll be..." She glanced awkwardly into his face, mere inches from her own.

"Yeah, the names of some of these things are pretty funny. Elbows, J-necks, close nipples, male and female connectors."

"Hmm." Lark scanned the page. "I suppose it could be worse."

"Ha. I guess so." Cole ruffled her hair.

They'd been working together all Saturday morning, trying to make some sense out of the mess Buford had left.

Luckily, Mrs. Spring had taken Molly so they could concentrate on the task at hand. They'd both agreed it would probably be a good idea to try doing some of the work themselves, considering they had no idea when—or even if—Buford was ever coming back.

Lark was relieved and happy when Cole had suggested they try their hand at putting his place back together the night Buford had left the note, over a week ago. At first she'd been reluctant to impose on him, but he'd insisted, saying that if they didn't do it, it wouldn't get done. And he couldn't very well stay with her forever, now, could he?

With a niggling sense of sadness, she had to agree. No, he couldn't stay with them forever.

Every night since then they'd spent some time going over the different instruction manuals, organizing their plan of attack. And every night they'd grown closer and enjoyed each other's company more. It was so much more fun working with Cole than going it alone, Lark admitted to herself. Cole had a knack for mechanical things and seemed to be able to fill in technically what Lark had to offer creatively. They were a good team. Besides, they figured, they could always call a plumber if they were unable to do the job themselves. And who knew... Buford might even decide to show up again and take over.

In the meantime, Lark was relishing the time spent with Cole every bit as much as her daughter was.

"Okay. Think you can remember this?" Cole pointed to the list of plumbing terms listed on the page that now lay across the top of Lark's stomach. "We need two three-inch nipples...."

Lark nodded. "Check."

"One six-inch nipple, one J-neck, a handful of elbows and a couple of couplers, several eight-foot lengths of ABS pipe and some joint compound. Got that?"

"Check."

"Good." Wrapping his arms around her back, he proceeded to slide them out from inside the cabinet where they'd been laying. "Let's get going. If we hurry, we can make it to Buford's uncle's hardware store before it closes."

"This ought to be interesting," Lark sighed, as Cole hauled her to her feet.

"Oh, you're gonna love it," he assured her, with a push toward the front door. "We'll take your big farm rig."

"Only if you drive."

"Considering I just got my car back out of the shop and I'm still waiting for my new front window, you have a deal."

"Oh, shut up," she groused and punched him good-naturedly in the arm.

"This is it?"

"I guess so. The address is the same as the one in the phone book, anyway." Cole compared the paper he held in his hand with the numbers on the side of the building.

"It looks like a junkyard." Lark stared at the large sign tacked over the front door of what seemed to be an old brick warehouse. Beaumont's Hardware.

"Maybe it's different on the inside."

"You've never been here before?"

"No. I never even knew it existed until Buford mentioned his Uncle Pappy," Cole said, pulling the farm truck to a stop just outside the store. "If they don't have what we need, we can always head to Aurora. They have a big hardware store up there."

Lark smiled up at him as he helped her out of the truck. She was so glad he was here with her. Together, she was sure they could finish the job. With Cole at her side, she almost felt that she could tackle any project.

A bell clanked as they entered the musty old building. Gigantic piles of almost everything imaginable were stacked on the floor and stuffed into shelves that almost reached the ceiling. Aisle after aisle of the most amazing array of stuff Lark had ever laid eyes on cluttered the rooms. Lark and Cole exchanged dubious glances.

"Hello?" A thin, reedy voice called out from somewhere within the bowels of the store. A rustling sound moved toward them. "Someone there?"

"Uh, yes..." Lark responded, turning around to search for the person who belonged to the voice.

"Oh, there you are," he shouted. With a loud clatter, what appeared to be the proprietor of the establishment swung his cane in her direction, knocking over a stack of boxes in the process. "Hello there. Pappy Beaumont at your service."

Lark felt her jaw drop as a spry, bandy-legged, nearly blind man stumbled through the carnage of his store to where they stood. He had to be rapidly approaching his hundredth year, Lark was sure.

"What is it you're needin'?" he hollered, his dry voice cracking as he reached them. He pushed his clacking dentures away from his gums and sucked at them noisily.

"Plumbing supplies, sir," Lark responded, valiantly resisting the urge to reach out and steady the crazily swaying man. She looked up at Cole in concern.

The ancient man scratched the long, wispy gray hair that sprouted wildly from his head. "Jumping lines? Like for a car?"

"No," Cole corrected mildly. "Like pipes...?"

"Pipes?" he screamed, seeming to think that they were probably as hard of hearing as he was. He sucked his dentures thoughtfully. "Tobacco pipes? Bagpipes? What's your pleasure? I got 'em all."

Cole took a step forward and raised his voice loudly. "Plumbing pipes, sir."

"Plumbing pipes, huh? Well, why didn't you say so in the first place? We got pipes. If I don't have it, it doesn't exist," the crotchety old geezer proclaimed. Wielding his cane like a weapon, he whipped it around and pointed to several large piles toward the back of the store. "Now finding it..." he cackled dryly " . . . that's another story. Come on back."

Thankfully, Cole kept a tight grip on Lark's elbow, steadying her as they threaded their way through the maze that was Pappy's store. More than once she stumbled, relying on Cole's strong arms to hold her up. They exchanged amused glances as the old man used his cane like a machete, fighting his way through his jungle of odds and ends.

Jabbing at a mountain of boxes filled with plastic plumbing doodads, Pappy stopped and began his unsteady ascent. As they watched him climb, Lark gripped Cole's arm in alarm. "Should he be doing that?" she whispered in fear as the man swayed wildly to and fro.

Cole shrugged helplessly. "I don't know. He's lived a lot more years than I have, so I guess he knows what he's doing." Nevertheless, Cole moved into position to catch Pappy—just in case.

"This here's your plastic supplies," he shrieked, smacking the pile with the sole of his shoe. "Over there." He squinted across the room. "Is your copper parts and down in the basement under the spare organ pieces, I got your galvanized and a bunch of other stuff you might need. Anything in particular you're looking for?"

"J-necks and close nipples?" Cole asked, moving to a better angle to catch the old man.

"J-necks? Nipples? Say, you wouldn't be the young couple my nephew Buford's been working for, wouldja?" he shouted gleefully.

Lark blushed at his choice of words and the crimson in her cheeks intensified when Cole answered that, yes indeed, they were that couple.

He squinted thoughtfully at them. "You know," he yelled, "Buford went to visit his mama. My sister. Lives in Nawlins. He came by before he left and told me to take care of ya. I got Mondays off, so I can come give ya a hand." Waving his arms in sudden crazy circles, Pappy lost his balance and fell backward into the pile he'd been standing on.

"Here ya go." Laughing, Pappy held up a plastic J-neck and tossed it to Cole. He laughed and wheezed and wheezed and laughed until after a moment of silence Lark was afraid he'd passed away.

"Uh, Pappy?" Lark held her breath till he moved.

"Gack?" he hacked, squinting at her through watery eyes.

"Thanks for your kind offer to help on Monday, but I think we have it under control."

"Well, okay. But if you change your mind, just holler," he cackled and struggled to stand up.

She had to bite the inside of her cheek to keep from laughing as Cole grabbed her by the arm and hustled her downstairs into a sea of spare parts.

"Can't you just see him taking over where Buford left off?" Cole laughed, shaking his head incredulously. "No, I think I'd hire you, before I'd hire him."

"Thanks a bunch," she cried, feigning hurt feelings.

"Pipes?" Cole hollered gleefully, pinching her arm. "Why didn't you just say so?"

"Shh," she cautioned, laughing. "He'll hear you."

Cole raised a skeptical eyebrow. "Think so?"

"Well, maybe not..."

For the better part of an hour Lark and Cole wandered through the most truly amazing collection of spare thinga-majigs and whatchamacallits they'd ever had the pure childlike pleasure of exploring.

"Would you get a load of this!" Cole held up what looked like the underpants for a suit of armor.

"What is it?"

"I don't have a clue."

"Looks like a chastity belt to me," Lark mused, reaching up and running her hand across the cool metal.

Cole inspected it with a new gleam in his eye. "I wonder how much it is...?"

"Why, are you thinking about buying it?"

"Maybe."

"Don't worry," she chided him, taking the strange contraption out of his hands and setting it on the floor where he'd found it. "Your virtue is safe with me."

"Aww." Cole pushed his lower lip out petulantly. "You're no fun."

"Tough," she giggled. "And put that down," she ordered, as he picked up a tuba and brought it to his lips for an earsplitting sour note. "We're here to find plumbing supplies, remember?"

"Oh, c'mon. Just a little song I wrote for you," he cajoled, blowing noisily into the dented instrument.

The horrible racket tickled her funny bone and she had to sit down on the floor and hold her stomach. "Stop it," she howled. "You're hurting me." Doubling over with laughter, she tried to cover her ears with her knees.

Cole grinned mischievously. "Don't you like a good horn solo?"

"A good one, yes," she hooted with glee.

"No problem," he said, picking up a tambourine. "I'm multi-instrumental," he bragged, and banged the noisy disk on the top of his head.

"You're hopeless." Grabbing the tambourine out of Cole's hands, Lark pulled herself to her feet, tossed it back on the shelf and taking him firmly by the hand, led him over to the area where Pappy had told them they would most likely find what they needed.

After another half hour of vigorous searching, they finally found what they were looking for and were ready at last to leave Beaumont's Hardware.

"Find everything okay?" Pappy yelled, leaning across the counter and scrutinizing them through watery bloodshot eyes. He sucked his dentures with relish.

"Oh, yes," Lark assured him, helping Cole bag their booty after Pappy had rung them up on his ancient cash register.

"Well, hell now, that's a first. I can guaran-damn-tee ya most people can't find a thing in that mess down there." He wheezed and laughed and gasped for air, once again causing Lark's heart to skip several beats. "You kids come back now, ya hear? It's been a pleasure doin' business with ya."

"Are you hungry?"

"I'm getting there. Why?"

Lark, lying spoon fashion with Cole under the kitchen cabinet, rested the hand that held the flashlight on the floor. "Because I thought if you could spare me, I'd get out of here and fix us some dinner."

His arm snaked around her waist and tightened, holding her in place. "Don't move," he instructed. "We're almost there."

Lark sighed. She knew she shouldn't be enjoying this quite so much, but try as she might she couldn't seem to help herself. Snuggling against Cole, even in the dank interior of a moldy old cabinet, excited her far more than was appropriate for a landlord and tenant working on a simple plumbing problem together. Yes. She needed to make dinner soon. And not because she was hungry for food.

"That's it," Cole announced, tying the new pipes to the wall with pipe strap. "Phase one, completed."

"Really?" Lark asked, delighted. "You're wonderful."

"No, not really," Cole teased and patted her hip affectionately. "Merely incredibly talented. Although I must give you some of the credit. You hold a mean flashlight."

"It's all in the wrist," she said demurely. "Now, how about if I rustle us up some chow?"

Before she could escape the confines of the kitchen cabinet, Cole gripped her arm and turned her slightly to face him. "I have a better idea."

"Oh?"

"Yeah. Why don't I take you out to dinner? And then maybe a movie."

Little jolts of excitement shot through Lark at his suggestion. That sounded heavenly. She hadn't been out to dinner with a man in years. "What about Molly?"

"Tonight, I'm more interested in Molly's mother." His eyes searched her face, landing on her mouth. "Why don't you call Mrs. Spring and ask if she'd be willing to sit with Molly tonight?"

Knowing she should resist temptation and spend a quiet evening of quality time with her daughter, Lark was surprised to hear herself say, "Deal."

"Good," Cole grinned down at her from where he'd propped himself over her shoulder inside the cabinet. "You go take care of that and I'll clean up here. Then let's get gussied up and go somewhere nice to celebrate."

"Celebrate what?"

"A successful day of plumbing, of course."

"Good idea. Better celebrate now, while we have the chance. Tomorrow it could all blow up in our faces."

Standing in front of her closet, Lark surveyed her meager wardrobe. What exactly did Cole mean by gussied up? Ben had never been the type to take his wife out on the town, and her fundamental clothing reflected that life-style. The only thing she owned that would even remotely work was the violet wool jersey. She loved the soft feel of the fabric and the way it matched the color of her eyes. She only hoped Cole would like it.

Piling her hair on top of her head, she fastened the cubic zirconia earrings Ben had given her for their last anniversary. She'd known they weren't real, but she loved the way they sparkled. A touch of lipstick and mascara, some powder for her nose, a bit of blush for her cheeks, and slipping into her pumps, she was ready.

Taking a deep breath to steady her suddenly nervous stomach, she headed to the stairs.

Cole was pacing back and forth at the bottom of the staircase, feeling uncomfortable in the sport coat he seldom had occasion to wear. Pushing his almost shoulder-length hair back from his face, he wondered again if this was such a good idea. It wasn't a date, but it sure felt like it. And he wasn't ready to date. No way. Dating led to courtship, courtship led to marriage, marriage led to divorce and broken hearts.

He groaned out loud. He should have told Lark to get Molly and that he'd treat them to dinner at the Mousey Cheese or whatever the hell the name of that kiddy pizza parlor was. Molly was a great chaperon. So far, she'd made it easy for him not to storm troop Lark's door in the middle of the night and show her how much he was beginning to care.

"I'm ready."

At the sound of her low, sexy voice, Cole spun around to see Lark standing at the bottom of the stairs looking like something out of a magazine. Her violet dress brought out the iridescent beauty of her eyes. The clingy outfit molded with little subtlety to her small, curvy frame and the heels she wore brought out the shapeliness of her perfect legs. She was truly the most beautiful woman he had ever laid eyes on. And best of all, she'd just announced that she was ready. Ready. Ready or not . . .

"You look fabulous," he breathed, not trusting himself to elaborate.

"Thanks," she murmured, lowering her heavily fringed eyes. "Shall we go?"

He felt himself nodding dumbly. "Ready." Tucking her hand in the crook of his arm, he led her out the door to his car.

Chapter Nine

"Does she always sleep this soundly?" Cole asked as he held Molly, who was floppy as a rag doll, over Lark's bed. They had just returned from picking the little girl up at the baby-sitter's.

Smiling, Lark pulled the comforter back so that Cole could slip Molly under the covers. "Yes. Once she's asleep, she's out. Sometimes I think she could sleep on a picket fence." She folded the blankets under the child's small chin and stood back with Cole to look down at the angelic face. "She's had a hard night of banging on Mrs. Spring's piano and singing her heart out."

Cole grinned. "Where does she get some of those lyrics?"

"I've often wondered that myself. I really think she believes she's singing the right words." Lark returned his grin. "It's not just song lyrics, either. She called our neighbor's crop duster a crap buster ever since she could talk ... things like that. I don't have the heart to correct her."

"She's a pretty special kid," Cole said, and reached down to smooth a brick-colored curl away from the small mouth, slack with sleep. He was only beginning to comprehend how much he'd missed out on with his son, Jake.

"Umm." Lark nodded lovingly down at the sleeping girl. Turning to Cole she whispered, "I was just going to make a cup of tea. Would you care to join me?"

He knew he should probably go stuff his lanky frame into the sardine can that was his bed, but he wasn't ready for his evening with Lark to be over just yet.

"Sure. Sounds great," he agreed in a hushed voice, as he followed her down the stairs. When she reached the bottom, she kicked off her pumps and breezed artlessly into the kitchen, motioning for him to join her.

As he sat at the kitchen table, watching her boil water and fill a plate with cookies, he tried to remember the last time he'd enjoyed an evening so much. He couldn't. Oh, he'd dated now and then in the years since his divorce, thanks to Randy, but always with lukewarm-to-disastrous results. No one had ever affected him the way Lark had. There was something about her that could make him feel every emotion from *A* to *Z* with an intensity that left him shaking in his boots. Bad or good, at least with Lark he felt alive.

"Thank you for the lovely dinner," she said, handing him a steaming mug of tea. Collecting her own mug, she sat down across from him at the table and smiled. "It was such a nice change of pace. I really never get a chance to go out."

Her admission had his heart singing. For some dumb reason, he was inordinately happy that it was he and he alone who constituted her dating life. "Anytime," he said and meant it. He wanted to start getting out a little more himself. "What did you think of the movie?"

"The movie?" she squeaked, suddenly staring at something fascinating in the bottom of her cup. "It was...I, uh...what did you think?"

He studied her face, wondering how he should respond. After all, the movie had been her choice. He was no prude, and with a title like *Naked Attraction,* he should have had some sort of clue as to what they were in for, but nothing had prepared him for the sheer...nakedness.

He cleared his throat and studied his nails. "The photography was good."

Lark nodded, biting her lower lip and seeming more interested than ever in the goings-on at the bottom of her cup. "Yes," she agreed glancing up toward the vicinity of his collar. "It really seemed to capture the flavor..." her eyes darted to his and back to her cup "...I mean the moment...or...moments there."

She was right. And there had been many moments to capture. Endless moment after moment of every style and variation of lovemaking imaginable were montaged together to zip up a practically nonexistent plot. It had been torture sitting there in the dark, with Lark and all that heavy breathing. It made hand-holding or a few innocent kisses next to impossible. What would she have thought if he'd slipped his arm around her while some guy on the screen hopped from bed to bed?

He wanted to seem as macho and hip as the next guy, but frankly, for a first date anyway, he'd have preferred a few less body parts and a lot more story.

"Actually," he admitted, squeezing out his tea bag and setting it on the table, "I'm more of an action-adventure kind of guy. Bond is more my speed."

"Really?" she breathed, smiling up into his eyes. "Me, too."

"Yeah. How did you hear about *Naked Attraction,* anyway?"

"I didn't." She looked up at him, surprised. "I just assumed it was one of those slapstick lampoon-type movies."

"Oh," he laughed. "Well, next time we want comedy, we'll have to read the reviews."

Pleased that there might be a next time, Lark giggled. "Okay. I'll admit that after about the ninth or tenth, umm . . . love scene, I wanted to start laughing."

Cole hooted. "You, too? Hey, what was with those three French maids and that gigolo? What was that all about?"

"Oh, please." The mirth bubbled up in her throat. "Okay, and how come that was the only scene that those four people were even in? Where did they come from? Where did they go?"

He laughed along with her. "I think they edited in a scene from another movie altogether. Come to think of it, all the scenes were sort of like that."

"Except for that one really big woman who kept showing up. I never could figure out who she was."

"The one with terminal PMS? I think she was the bad guy."

"Oh." Lark tried to control her giggling before she took a sip of tea. It was no use, so giving in to her laughter, she put the cup down and pushed it out of harm's way. "Who was the good guy?"

"Well," Cole lifted a mischievous eyebrow. "According to that tall, dark guy with the fedora, they were all pretty good."

"Some better than others," she agreed, as Cole reached across the table and playfully squeezed her hand.

As Lark settled in next to Molly that night, she was still smiling. Everything about her day with Cole had been per-

fect. Even the arguments. And as much as she'd vowed to
remain emotionally detached, Cole was making it very
tough. Handsome, charismatic, thoughtful, generous,
hardworking, smart...

Sighing, she turned over on her side and watched Molly's little chest rise and fall in the moonlight. She knew it
was unfair to compare Ben to Cole, but Ben was all she'd
ever known as far as relationships went and Cole suited her
in ways she hadn't even known a man could suit her. It was
as if they were of one mind at times.

The frightening possibility that she might be falling in love
with her professor flitted through her mind, but she managed to push it away. No, that couldn't be it. She'd promised herself she wouldn't let something like this happen. And
so, she thought—taking a deep breath and stroking Molly's
smooth alabaster cheek—she wouldn't.

Over the next weeks, whenever Lark and Cole weren't in
school or preparing for class, they were home working on
the duplex. Countless trips to Pappy's and endless referrals
to the home-improvement books kept them moving forward quite nicely.

The aged plumbing in both apartments had all been replaced. The wiring, with the help of one of Cole's faculty
friends, had been completely updated and now met all safety
standards and county inspection codes. Rotting studs and
floor joists had been replaced with new lumber, hauled back
from the lumberyard in Lark's old flatbed. The roof
sported—for the first time in years—handsome composi-
tion shingles, installed by a reasonably priced roofing crew,
and the pieces of gutter that Cole hadn't been able to
straighten and patch had been replaced. New drywall covered the holes Buford had chopped in the walls and the un-
fortunate doorway Cole had created between their places.

Soon they'd be finished taping and texturing and could begin painting the rooms in Cole's place.

Molly had enjoyed the whole procedure immensely, thrilled and honored to act as Cole's assistant until her bedtime each night. And since there was always time to stop for a quick airplane or horsey ride, she rarely got bored with the remodeling process.

The time spent together served only to seal the bond that all three of them had been forming, until—though neither Cole nor Lark would admit it—they couldn't envision the day when Cole would actually move back to his place.

"Is this right?" Lark asked, troweling some plaster into a nail hole in the drywall. It was nearly midnight and Cole was trying to teach her the fine art of mudding and taping.

Cole moved behind her shoulder and watched. "No, not that much. You're not decorating a cake here."

She giggled.

"More like this," he instructed, guiding her trowel at a low angle across a few of the seams and nail holes in the area where she was working. Resting his left hand lightly on her waist, he moved her right arm up and down, literally dancing her across the wall.

She began to hum in time to his even, powerful strokes. "Where did you learn to do this? The Arthur Murray School of Drywall?"

Chuckling, Cole dipped her back in his arms and loaded her trowel with another scoop of mud. "Actually," he teased, cha-chaing her back to the wall, "I learned drywalling when I was a kid, working for a construction crew during summer vacation."

"So," Lark giggled, "was the foreman a good dancer?"

"She was excellent," he growled, nuzzling her ear playfully.

"Aha! So you have done this with another woman."
Tucking her chin into her shoulder, she looked back at him
with mock disdain. "You tramp."

"That's me," he said affably, whirling her back toward
the mud bucket. "But she was nowhere near as cute as you
are. She didn't have your adorable nose." He smeared a
dollop of plaster across her nose. "Or your smooth, rosy
cheeks." Another glob of mud for each cheek. "Or your
swanlike neck." A handful of mud disappeared down the
front of her blouse.

"Is that so?" Lark asked calmly, scooping a glob of mud
out of the front of her bra and shoving it in his ear. "How
about my delicate shell-like ears?"

"Nooo, I can't say that she did . . ." Cole laughed, as he
dug the plaster out of his ear.

Turning in Cole's arms, Lark rubbed her nose and cheeks
on his neck. It didn't matter. Their hair and clothes were
already covered in the stuff anyway.

"Thanks," she said airily, trying to still her pounding
heart. "I think I have the hang of it now." Disentangling
herself from his arms, she backed up toward her work area.

This man was too potent for his own good. Ever since that
kiss in Molly's room the night he'd moved in, Lark had been
trying her level best to stay out of his embrace. There was a
danger there that threatened her well-laid plans for the future.

As it was, she knew there would be emotional hell to pay
when they finished this project and Cole moved back to his
side of the duplex. She didn't want to make his leaving any
harder on herself or Molly than it had to be. Unfortunately, there was a little voice in the back of her mind
taunting her with the fact that it was already too late. Ignoring this voice, she attacked the wall with renewed vigor.

"That's good," he praised, just over her shoulder. "You've got it now."

She could feel his warm, sexy breath tickle the side of her neck and his after-shave tantalized her nose. Back off, she wanted to shout, for self-preservation. Can't you see what you're doing to me? But knowing that would probably only compound the problem, she changed the subject.

"Cole?"

"Hmm?" His hot breath scalded her cheek.

Just how close did he have to stand? She couldn't take much more. She moved away once again. "Uh, you know that midterm in your class next week?"

"Umm-hmm. What about it?"

His breath was minty fresh. How'd he do it? "Well, I need to do really well in my computer and accounting classes, because I want to get a job as a bookkeeper this summer, so I can, you know..." she scooped another glob of mud onto her trowel " ... keep us fed."

"Umm-hmm," he breathed over her shoulder, scrutinizing her work. "You missed a spot," he whispered, pointing at the wall. "Continue," he commanded, fanning the little hairs at the nape of her neck.

"It's just that..." she took a deep breath "...I don't just want to pass, I want to be perfect. I don't know exactly why, but it's important to me. I have something to prove to myself, I guess."

He nodded, removing the trowel from her hand and fixing a seam she'd muffed. "Understandable."

"So, anyway, could you give me a hint? Will it be hard?"

Cole grinned down at her, popping the tool back into her hand. "Yes. But stop worrying. It's not fatal. If you know the text and the lecture material, you'll be fine. No one ever gets all the questions right. I throw a few curveballs in for fun, but that shouldn't affect your final score. Hey, if you

can pass my class with only U-bank experience, then you'll
be doing swell."

Lark's brow puckered with worry. "Really?"

"Yup."

"Okay. If you say so." Turning, she looked up into his
baby blue eyes and felt herself begin to melt. Time to escape to the safety of her own room. "Maybe we should call
it a night, huh? It's after midnight and..." she grinned
winsomely up at him "...I have a test to study for."

"Oh, hi, Randy. Just a second and I'll get Cole.... Yeah,
sure, what?" Lark tucked the phone between her ear and
shoulder and glanced back at Cole, who had suddenly
stopped eating his breakfast to look at her. "Umm-hum.
Umm-hum. Umm-hum..."

Cole frowned. Something about the tone of her voice in-
trigued him. What on earth could they be talking about?
Molly blew bubbles in her milk with a straw, till annoyed,
Cole shushed her. He couldn't hear what Lark was saying.

"Ah, well, gee... Is it Friday already? I, uh..." Her eyes
darted nervously around the room as she listened to Cole's
best friend speak. "Nothing really. No, uh, just a few things
around here. But," she muttered, "I should probably, you
know, stay here and work...."

In an effort to seem uninterested in her conversation, Cole
loaded his mouth with way too much cereal and tried to look
blasé. Her laughter tinkled girlishly at something his skirt-
chasing friend said, and Cole's spine began to stiffen. Just
what the heck was lover boy telling her?

"Oh, Randy," she giggled. "You're so weird. No. I guess
I don't have any excuses. Okay, it sounds like fun. I, uh, will
have to get a sitter for Molly though...."

The child groaned, echoing Cole's instincts. He knew how
she felt.

Pouting, Molly looked up at Cole. "I don't want to go to the sitter."

"I know, kid." He smiled sympathetically. "How would you feel about a piece of toast with jam?" He had to busy himself with something other than Lark's phone conversation.

"Okay." Swinging her feet, she began blowing bubbles into her milk again. Just as well. If Lark wanted him to know what Randy had said, she'd probably tell him.

Lark hung up the phone to find Cole around the corner, cursing the two charcoal disks he'd finally managed to dislodge from her finicky toaster. Trying not to smile, she waited until the smoke had cleared before she approached him about her date with his friend.

Randy had caught her completely off guard. She'd had no excuse not to go out with him, she thought irritably, as Cole hadn't bothered reserving any time with her since they'd gone out together several weeks earlier. Just as well. This was the perfect way to prove to herself and to Cole that she was not growing too dependent on him. It was just a little dinner party, anyway. Randy's original date had taken ill at the last minute. How could she refuse?

"Need any help?"

"No," he barked, tossing the toast like two black Frisbees into the trash, where a tail-wagging AWOL immediately rooted them out and chased them around the floor. Turning to her, his smile was brittle. "Who was on the phone?"

As if he didn't know. "Randy."

"Oh? What did he want?"

Nudging him aside, Lark dug two fresh pieces of bread out of the plastic wrapper and popped them into the toaster. "Actually, he called to ask me out to dinner tonight."

"Oh?" His smile was still flash frozen on his face, making her nervous. "What'd you say?"

"Yes."

"Ah."

"He kind of caught me off guard, there," she explained weakly, feeling like a naughty little kid. She didn't like the feeling. Avoiding his piercing gaze, she began to clean off the counter and load the sink with dishes. "I figured we could use a break from this project for a while, anyway. Right?"

"You did." His voice was flat.

She glanced up at his wooden expression as she came back to the toaster. Ejecting the toast before it could begin to burn, Lark kept her hands busy. She had the sudden urge to slug Cole in the arm. Why was he acting this way? She wasn't trying to steal his best friend, for crying in the night. It was just a simple dinner party. And if she wanted to take the evening off from this sweatshop, she damn well could. It would do them both good.

"Yes. I did. Why?"

He shrugged, lifting a disapproving eyebrow. "I was under the impression that you wanted to finish up my apartment so that I would have a place to live."

You have a place to live, she wanted to shout. "I do. What I don't see is what difference one little evening will make."

Cole sighed and shook his head, still oozing that parental censure that irked her. "None, I guess."

"Well, good," she said, handing him two perfectly toasted pieces of bread. "Now, if you don't mind, I have to go call Mrs. Spring about watching Molly tonight."

"She doesn't want to go to the sitter."

She glanced over at Molly. "Well, that's just too bad, now, isn't it?"

Raking a tired hand over his unshaven jaw, he mumbled, "I'll watch her."

"You will?" She stared in surprise as he ambled over and tossed a piece of toast on her daughter's plate.

"Sure. Isn't that right, pardner?" Sinking coolly onto his seat, he began to butter his toast.

"Yeah!" Molly yelled and waved her hands happily in the air.

"I love you! You love me!"

Sitting on the couch next to Cole, Molly grinned happily up at him and sang along with a videotape. It had to be the fiftieth time that evening he'd been treated to the song and he was beginning to lose his mind.

Although, to be honest with himself, the reason he was so uptight was the fact that it was after midnight and there was still no sign of Lark. As the song came to an end, Cole looked down into the winsome freckled face.

"Okay, pardner, time to hit the hay."

Molly frowned petulantly. "But my mom said I could stay up till she got home."

"True." Cole nodded, feeling rather crabby himself. "But what she didn't say was that she'd be out this late. It's way, way, way past your bedtime." It was way past his bedtime, too.

"Aww," she moaned, folding her arms across her tummy.

"C'mon, now. Is that anyway for a pardner to act?"

The child grinned. "Will you horsey-ride me upstairs?"

Cole leaned down so that she could climb up onto his shoulders. "Sure, little gal. I'll even gallop ya once or twice around the corral here, just for fun."

"Yippee! Giddyap!" she screamed, and filling her hands with his long, blond hair she nudged him in the ribs with her feet. "Let's go shoot the bad guys."

"Sounds like a plan," Cole thought grimly, as he trotted the child off to dreamland.

An hour later, Cole found himself still waiting for Lark's return. Why hadn't he staked his claim on Lark before? he wondered, mentally kicking himself for letting Randy get his toe in the door with her. He should have asked her out himself. It's just that they'd been so busy. Striding to the window, he peeked out to the front porch for the third time in less than a minute. Hang it all, as soon as she came back tonight he was going to take care of that little detail. Somehow.

Somehow, without scaring her off, he had to let her know that he could take care of her out-to-dinner needs. Given half a chance, he'd like to take care of a lot more than that in her life.

The time since he'd put Molly in Lark's bed seemed to slip excruciatingly by. He was starting to climb the walls in earnest. What the hell was going on? Had they been in a car wreck? Were they all right? Should he start calling the hospitals? The cops? Had Randy seduced her? Should he start polishing the shotgun?

Raking his hands roughly through his already disheveled locks, he growled and flopped down on Lark's hideous old couch and wondered if the National Guard was listed in the Yellow Pages.

A low giggle filtered through the front door. It was followed by some hushed conversation and low laughter. Lark was home. Randy, too, by the sound of it.

Not wanting to appear overly concerned or interested, Cole leaned back on the couch and pretended to be asleep. More laughter and whispering wafted just outside his ability to understand what they were talking about. What was taking so long? he wondered grumpily, already tired of pretending to be asleep.

Cole glanced at his watch. They'd been standing there for a quarter of an hour now. Another giggle. More hushed conversation. He was going crazy. Unable to stand it any longer, he leapt to his feet and strode to the door. Yanking it open he was amazed to find his best friend kissing Lark good-night.

Jealousy, unlike any he'd ever experienced before, seared through his gut. This was worse than Sherry and the Goody Bar Man. This was betrayal by the two people he cared most about in the world. And just because one of them had no clue how he felt was no damned excuse.

He knew his face must be flaming with anger, as they both stood there staring at him so strangely. He didn't care. He'd been cheated. Been mistreated.

"Hey," he yelled into the hushed silence of the wee morning hours. "Keep it down out here. People are trying to sleep."

And on that eternally humiliating note, he slammed the door shut in their mutually stunned faces.

Chapter Ten

Locking the door behind her, Lark came into the house to find Cole standing at the kitchen sink staring out the window.

"What is your problem?" she asked, taking in the grim set of his jaw and the deep grooves he'd finger-combed into his hair.

Turning a bleary eye on her, he watched her come in and lean against the counter several feet away. He attempted to appear nonchalant. "Problem?"

So that's the way he wanted to play it. Well, it was late and she was cranky now, thanks to him. She would just save everyone a little time and cut to the chase.

"Out there. Just now. The raving lunatic at the door."

Cole snorted. "I'm not the one with the problem."

She threw up her hands in exasperation. "Oh? And I suppose I am?"

"Hey." His head snapped up and he glared angrily at her. "You could have called. Molly was getting worried." That wasn't exactly true, but he figured he could use a little dose of parental guilt to his advantage.

Lark frowned. "Where is she?"

"In bed, asleep," he said defensively. "She wanted to stay up until you got home, but since I wasn't sure if you were even going to come home tonight, I finally had to put her to bed." He pinned her with an accusing glare.

Gasping, Lark turned an outraged face to him. "Is that what you think of me? That I would stay out all night? On a first date? On any date for that matter, without even calling?" Her voice rose more shrilly with each question.

No. That's not exactly what he'd thought, but he had to wonder what was going on. Especially after what he'd just seen. "Okay, Ms. Goody Two Shoes, just what the heck went on at *dinner* that took so long, anyway? You must have had time for at least a twelve-course meal." This was coming out all wrong. He was sounding like some kind of nagging boyfriend. He didn't want to stand here and fight with her. Weren't they past all this?

What he really wanted to do was claim her as his exclusive dinner partner and then kiss the hell out of her.

After that, if he was feeling really adventurous, he might even gather up his nerve and reveal the fact that he'd been married before and had a son. It was about time he told her, and he'd thought she was the type of person he could trust with something like that. But after what he'd just seen at the front door, he was beginning to have his doubts.

And now his best friend was in the picture. His blood began to boil all over again. "Did he try anything? Because if he did, I'm going to..."

Lark's head throbbed. This was getting preposterous. "I don't have to listen to this," she said angrily and pushed past him toward the dining room.

"He did, didn't he?" Following right behind, Cole shook furious fists at the ceiling.

Spinning on her heel, Lark stopped so abruptly she nearly knocked Cole over. "No. He did not."

"Hey, I have eyes. I saw the two of you kissing out there." He winced. He was really starting to sound like an idiot, but for the life of him, he couldn't stop.

"You need glasses, you big, dumb jerk. You saw one of us kissing out there, and it wasn't me. He kissed me on the cheek to thank me for helping him out tonight. That's it. Nothing more. Not," she said churlishly, her eyes narrowing, "that it's any of your business."

"Ha!" he shouted. "I'll damn well make it my business! What goes on under my roof with my best friend and my... my..." he stuttered, searching for the word that would describe her relationship to him. That was the problem. There wasn't one. At some point it had all become much too complex to define with a simple word.

Lark looked up sharply. "Your roof? Since when is it *your* roof?"

Oh, for crying in the night, was she going to argue semantics? Now? When he was busy trying to stake his stupid claim? He inhaled deeply and tried to rein in his raging temper before lashing out again. "As long as I pay the rent around here, it *is* my roof and I have some say-so about what goes on under it. Especially when it concerns people I...I..."

Staring furiously at the wall, she waited for him to continue. "Yes?" She tapped her foot with impatience.

"Care about," he raged, and planted his hands squarely on his hips, as if daring her to defy him.

Her eyes slowly traveled to his. It took a moment for his words to sink in. He cared about her? Is that what he was saying? Is that what this was all about, she wondered. "You're jealous?"

"No," he snapped defensively. Oh, what the hell. She was going to find out sometime, anyway. "Yes."

"Really?"

She didn't have to look so pleased. "Yeah." Dragging his hands through his hair, he exhaled tiredly.

Moving toward him she looked deeply into his eyes, as if searching for the truth. Slowly, a smile stole across her lips.

Cole could feel his mouth involuntarily follow suit.

They stood there for the longest moment, absorbing what had just transpired, smiling at each other, happy, relieved and wondering what would happen next.

AWOL, returning from some foreign trek, lumbered noisily across the wooden floor and standing on hind legs threw her forepaws across Cole's chest and kissed him soundly on the lips.

"My sentiments exactly," Lark said, before she turned her back on the stunned professor and headed up the stairs to join her daughter in bed.

"I don't think I can hold it any longer!" Lark's fingers shrieked in agony as she pushed the heavy light fixture higher in her arms.

"Just give me another sec, darlin'," Cole mumbled, his mouth filled with wire nuts, as he hovered precariously above her on the ladder.

"I'm...uff...trying," she grunted, the fixture slipping slowly back down her arm, taking a chunk of flesh with it.

They were hanging a beautiful new brass-and-glass light fixture, suspended by a long chain, over Cole's stairway. The job was very tedious, somewhat dangerous, and he needed her help. It was one of the finishing touches they had to accomplish before his place was ready to move into.

"Done," he announced proudly, climbing down the ladder and taking the fixture out of her hands. "Good job, sport." Brushing his lips lightly across her forehead, he climbed back up the ladder with the fixture and hung the light, swag style, from a hook.

"Oh," Lark breathed, standing back to look. "It's beautiful."

"Just wait till I turn it on." Hopping down to the floor, he ran to the new electrical panel and turned on the breaker.

Reflected light danced across the walls, as the sparkling glass and brass captivated Lark.

"You are a genius," she said, turning to him with wide eyes.

Cole laughed and shook his head. "Yeah, right."

"No. Really. I think that's very sexy. I mean, that you can do that. I love a man in a tool belt."

Sweeping her into his arms, he kissed her soundly on the lips.

"What's next?" he asked, glancing around for the next project she had lined up.

"Nothing." She smiled up at him. "You're off for the day."

"Why?"

"Have you forgotten? Tomorrow is the big day."

"What big day?"

She tugged playfully at the front of his shirt. "The test, you big goof. Don't tell me you've forgotten your own test? I have to go study for it now."

"Oh, that. That's no big deal. It's just the midterm."

"I don't care. I want to be perfect." Pouting prettily, she stood on tiptoe and kissed his cheek.

His blue eyes darkened. "You already are."

Shaking her head, she backed out of his arms. "Not yet. But I will be. I'm going to go study."

"Okay." He watched her skip down his stairs. "Uh, Lark?"

"Yeah?" Pausing at the bottom, she looked up.

"Tomorrow night after the midterm let's go out to dinner. To celebrate?"

She dimpled happily. "I'd love to."

"Great. I...uh, have something to tell you." It was time to come clean about his past. To get over the Sherry-and-Jake stumbling block that had kept him from growing close to anyone for years.

Her brow puckered slightly for a moment. "Okay," she said uncertainly.

"It's no big deal, just something I've been meaning to talk to you about."

"Tomorrow night," she smiled, and skipped next door to her place to cram for his exam.

That did it. He needed a shrink. Cole stood in the middle of Molly's room the next morning, scratching his head in annoyance. Where on earth was his backpack? Everything he needed to administer the midterm to his C.S. 101 class that morning, was in that pack. Everything. The tests. The answer key. A pile of freshly sharpened No. 2 pencils for the boneheads who came without...

Getting down on his knees he stuck his head under the bed, only to be assailed by Molly.

"Yippee, I have a yo-yo. Yippee yea, yippee yea!" she sang loudly, as she climbed up onto his back.

"Dammit, Molly," he snapped, coming out from under the bed and dragging her off his back. "Knock it off, will you?"

Lower lip trembling, her eyes filled with tears as she stared up at him in surprise.

Oh great. "Hey, c'mere, kiddo."

He held his arms out to her and she came to him, soaking the front of his shirt with embarrassed tears.

"I'm sorry, pardner. I've had kind of a rough morning, and I'm in a real hurry. I didn't mean to hurt your feelings. How about I give you a big, long airplane ride before you go over to Mrs. Spring's tonight?"

Grinding her chubby fists into her eyes, she nodded up at him, her dimples appearing at the sides of her lips. "Okay," she whispered and crawled off his lap.

"Okay," he whispered back, as she left the room. Sinking down on her bed, he moaned in frustration. He had the whole thing loaded on disk in the computer-science department at school. If he hurried, he'd just have time to print and copy a whole new set.

One of these days he was going to get his act together.

Lark pulled on her jacket and strode to the front of the class, her test paper in hand.

She felt a little self-conscious, being the first one finished. Maybe she should have stayed in her seat for a while longer, to check over her answers. No. It was finally over. She'd done what she knew how to do, and it was a relief to have it out of the way.

Cole looked up in surprise as she handed him her paper with a saucy grin.

"That was quick." He glanced at the paper in his hand.

"I've been studying. I'll see you tonight," she whispered, glancing around the room to see if anyone was watching or listening. She didn't want to be labeled the teacher's pet.

"You got it." He winked and watched her walk out the door.

When she got outside the building, she walked briskly to her truck and sat behind the wheel. "Well, I did it, Ben," she said, feeling the need to sort out some feelings with her late husband. "I just took my first college exam. How about that? I'm..." she shrugged, looking over at the passenger seat, envisioning him there "... kind of proud of myself."

Shifting her eyes, she stared out the window at the overcast day and watched the bare tree branches bob and sway in the breeze.

"Oh, Ben." She sighed heavily. She didn't know how to tell him what she was feeling. That she was ready to forgive him for leaving her and Molly in such dire straits. For causing her so much grief with his wild dreams and schemes.

"You know in my way, I loved you very much. And I thank God every day for Molly. I just wanted you to know... that I'm happy now. Ready to move on with my life."

A lone tear trickled down her cheek.

"Ready to begin again." She wiped at the tear with her sleeve. "I'm finally happy, Ben. Really happy. And...I..." another tear followed the first "... just hope you can be happy for me, too."

The cab grew suddenly warmer as the sun peeked out from behind the clouds, filling the interior, bathing Lark in a golden glow.

Smiling through her blurry eyes, she looked up to the sky and smiled. "Oh, thanks, honey," she murmured and exhaled with a relieved shudder. "Thanks."

Leaning back in the chair at his desk in the computer-science department, Cole let his head fall back and stared up at the ceiling in shock.

He just couldn't believe it.

Out of fifty-six students in his C.S. 101 class, only one person had scored one hundred percent. Only one person had aced the test with flying colors, scoring perfectly on every question, including the tricks he'd thrown in for his own amusement.

And out of the entire class of fifty-six students, this person was the only person who'd never had any computer experience. Unless, of course, you counted the U-bank machine at the Piggly-Wiggly in Butteville . . .

Lark.

No one else even came close. Not even the brightest stars in class.

Icy cold fingers of nausea crawled up his throat. He was going to be sick. He couldn't believe what a fool he'd been. Again. Raking his hands through his long, shaggy hair, he stood and crossing the room threw open a window, where he gulped in huge lungfuls of cool autumn air.

Sick, angry and hurting, Cole could only surmise that since Lark was the only person on campus to have access to the test and the answer key, she'd taken his backpack and cheated.

He'd been cheated. . . . One more damn time. What an idiot. He was beyond disgust with himself for allowing this to happen. What prompted him to fall in love with cheating, lying, conniving women? Women who would stop at nothing to get what they wanted.

Angrily, he stuffed the tests into a paper bag—since he no longer had a briefcase or backpack—and locked his office door behind him as he left.

It was time for a little chat with his landlord. No one played Cole Richardson for a fool. Especially not a woman he would ever consider marrying.

* * *

Humming, Lark squirted a line of mustard down the hotdog bun she was preparing for Molly's dinner. She wished she had something else to wear tonight other than her violet jersey dress. Cole had already seen her in that, and she wanted tonight to be something special.

A celebration in more than one sense of the word. She had so many things to be thankful for. The test was over, the duplex was shaping up nicely, she'd finally made her peace with Ben and she was getting along famously with Cole.

Better than famously. Fabulously famously.

She grinned. Life was wonderful.

As she fished Molly's hotdog out of boiling water and plopped it into its bun, she wondered absently what Cole wanted to tell her. He'd seemed so serious the previous night....

She could hear Molly in the living room as she met Cole at the front door.

"Hi yourself, pardner" was his reply to her silly greeting.

Their playful banter never ceased to bring an amused smile to her mouth. However, this time there was an edge to his tone. An edge that brooked no argument.

"Why don't you go on outside and find that big, old doggy of yours, okay? I need to talk to your mama for a little while."

"Okay," the child obediently complied, obviously reading the same message into his words.

Concerned, Lark stepped into the living room as her daughter headed for the porch.

"Hi," she offered tentatively, wondering what was wrong. He looked positively murderous. A current of fear skittered down her spine.

"Hi." His voice was flat as he stood studying her through veiled eyes.

Never one to stand on ceremony, Lark decided to take the bull by the horns. "What's wrong?"

Laughing humorlessly, Cole tossed the tests, the answer key and the class score sheet down on the coffee table in front of her broken-down sofa.

"You tell me," he challenged.

Sinking down to the lumpy seat, she gathered papers up and studied them with a puzzled frown. "I don't get it."

Emitting a sharp burst of laughter, his eyes clouded dangerously. "Lark, don't play dumb with me."

"Play dumb...what? I still don't get it." She stared harder at the pages in her hand.

Okay. He'd go along with her little game. For a while. "If you'll look at the class scores, you'll see that you are the only person in a class of fifty-six students to get a perfect score."

She looked at him with wide violet-eyed innocence. "Really? Wow," she murmured.

"Yeah. Wow. How about that?" His voice was literally dripping with sarcasm. He ambled slowly around the living room, watching as she glanced over the class score sheet. "Interesting, considering how you are the only one out of fifty-six people who'd never before touched a computer. Most of those people cut their teeth on a keyboard. But not you. Oh, no. You punch out a few dollars at the U-bank machine and suddenly you're my brightest student."

She looked up at him and shrugged, wondering where he was going with all this. She didn't have to wonder long. He was on a roll.

If looks could kill, she'd have been cremated by now.

"And isn't it fascinating how you were the only one with access to the answers. The missing answers, I might add."

Lark felt all the blood drain out of her face. Shaking, she dropped the papers she held to the coffee table in front of her and stared at him, stunned. "Missing?"

"Yeah." He had to admit, she was good with the innocent act. Sherry could take lessons from her. "Missing. Along with a lot of other papers and files that pertain to this class. Files and papers that have been missing since you moved in."

Unable to trust her voice, Lark cleared her throat and licked her dry lips. "Are you..." She choked and tried again. "Are you accusing me...of stealing?" Her eyes were round with shock and hurt. "Of...cheating?"

"Hey, if the backpack fits, baby."

"How dare you?" Lark had never been so outraged in her entire life. How was it that this man could bring out the extremes in her personality in less time than it took to detonate and explode a hand grenade? "I don't have to listen to this pile of crap," she snarled, keeping her voice low for Molly's benefit. "I studied hard for that grade and I earned it. If you believe I would stoop to cheating to pass your lousy, little computer class, then you can just go to hell."

She leapt to her feet and crossed the room to face him, her entire body shaking violently with rage. "I don't have anything to prove to you, *Professor* Richardson. Feel free to give me another test, written or verbal, anytime. Until then, you pompous jerk, get the hell out of my house."

"Gladly," he spat, and storming upstairs he grabbed an armload of his personal belongings from Molly's bedroom. Shirttails, sleeves, pant legs and shoelaces flying, he stumbled down Lark's stairs to the front porch, where with a vicious slam of his front door he disappeared into his place and out of hers forever.

Lark sank down on the front-porch stairs and sobbed.

Chapter Eleven

Lark's heart lurched into her throat at the sound of a knock at her front door. Cole? She checked her reflection in the hall mirror. Her eyes were red rimmed and puffy, her nose a bright pink and her usually creamy white complexion was blotchy.

She looked like an overripe tomato. But then, she'd been crying ever since Cole left that evening, so what did she expect? Threading her fingers through her hair, she attempted to straighten it out some on her way to the door. She didn't know why she made the effort. Cole obviously thought she was some kind of criminal. He wouldn't care if she looked like a derelict.

Lark opened the door to reveal a pipe-puffing Buford—his fingers hooked casually in the straps of his ever present overalls—standing on her front porch.

"Howdy, Ms. St. Clair."

"Buford!" Her eyes widened in surprise. He was the last

person she had expected to see. "Please . . ." she held open the screen door ". . . come in."

Shuffling slowly inside, Buford sank down into her easy chair and glanced around. "Looks like you been busy." He nodded in approval.

"Yes, we've gone ahead and picked up where . . ."

"Sorry I had to leave in such an all-fired hurry," he continued on, talking over the top of her. "But, I figured your job would wait. Mama wouldn't. She'll be a hundred on her next birthday, and when she calls I come a runnin'."

Lark simply nodded, figuring Buford wasn't interested in what she had to say, anyway.

"Yep. Sometimes in this life, you have to get the old priorities straight. Put loved ones first. Pride second." He puffed thoughtfully on his pipe for a moment. "That's what Mama always preaches anyway, and it seems to work for me. She always told me, 'Buford, life is too short to squander on things that just don't matter none.'" His eyes twinkled. "Not that your plumbin' ain't important. It's just not as important as Mama. Hope you understand."

She felt a lump grow in her throat at his words. Blinking back another torrent of tears, she sent him a bleary smile and nodded.

"Well." He struggled out of the easy chair to his feet. "It's past my dinnertime. I'll be back Monday next to tie up any loose ends around here for ya. Looks like the front porch could use some work, and that old paint job needs scraping and priming. Probably should do something about them cracks in your sidewalk, while I'm at it," he rambled, heading out the door without a backward glance. "Trees need limbing . . ."

Lark shut the door behind him and sagged wearily against the cool, hard surface.

* * *

Cole flailed around on the brand-new carpet that covered his bedroom floor and tried to get comfortable. No easy task, considering he didn't have any furniture or bedding. Pride prevented him from marching next door and pulling his mattress off Lark's back porch and over to his place.

Arranging several pairs of jeans up around his neck, he shivered in the darkness and longed for even the smallest of mattresses and a tiny iron bed. At least he'd be able to sleep.

No. He wouldn't. Not the way things stood now with Lark. Rolling over on his back, he covered his face with his hands. He couldn't even begin to reconcile all the emotions that had tortured him since he'd turned in that evening. Unable to concentrate on anything but his problems, he'd gone to bed—such as it was—at nine, and tossed and turned for the past three hours. According to his watch, it was after midnight.

He exhaled noisily.

How could he have been such a fool? She'd really hornswoggled him with her hardworking country-girl act. Talk about salt of the earth. Honest, trustworthy, loyal...all the Girl Scout attributes. He'd been so sure that she was different. And Molly. His heart turned over painfully at the thought of giving up the time he spent with his little pardner.

Punching the pile of shirts under his head into a more comfortable lump, he willed himself to go to sleep.

Laughing violet eyes and long, shapely legs kept intruding on his progress. What if he was wrong? What if she hadn't cheated? His eyes shot open in the dark and he stared, unseeing at the ceiling.

No. The evidence was too convincing.

"Damn!" Huffing in frustration, he rolled over on his stomach.

Okay. So she was guilty. Maybe he should forgive her and they could go back to the way things were....

"No," he yelled, flipping over to his back. He'd forgiven Sherry and the Goody Bar Man. Look where that had gotten him.

He punched the floor for emphasis.

The floor punched back.

That was strange. Had they forgotten to secure a floorboard? Tentatively, he hit the floor again and listened. This time the floor not only thumped back, it whimpered.

Whimpered?

Pressing his ear to the floor Cole could hear some sort of faint cries off in the distance. Not human cries, he noted, ruling out Molly and Lark with relief. He'd been right the first time. They were more like whimpers, mixed with sharp... yapping sounds? They seemed to be coming from directly under his floor.

What the devil could it be? Laying completely still, he could hear movement. A thumping of some sort. Didn't sound like a burglar, but it was hard to tell.

Flinging the pile of clothing off his body, Cole stood up and reached for his shoes. He'd never be able to sleep now, so he might as well go investigate. As quietly as he could, he went out to his car and rummaged around in his trunk till he found a flashlight and a tire iron. Safety first, he thought, gripping the cool iron tightly in his hand.

The moonlight filtered through the cloudy night, illuminating his path as he fought his way through the brambles to the backyard. Clicking on the flashlight, Cole directed its beam at the foundation of the house until he found what he was looking for. The crawl space.

He could tell he was on the right track, as the whimpering and yapping noises grew louder.

Geez, he hated crawling around in small, dank places during the day, let alone at midnight. Taking a deep breath, he sank down to his knees and trained the beam into the dark interior, praying that some rabid animal wouldn't come leaping out and eat his face.

Two reflective spots swung over toward him and held. Animal eyes, Cole surmised. Big animal eyes. His hand tightened convulsively around the tire iron. Shifting the light a little higher, the crawl space under the house was suddenly illuminated and Cole could see the animal in question.

AWOL.

She blinked at him and whined, licking her nose and waving at him with a forepaw. It was then he noticed them.

Puppies.

Nearly a half dozen of the cutest fluffballs Cole had ever seen, bellying up to AWOL's bar. They squealed and grunted greedily as they vied for position along her body and AWOL, seemingly exhausted by the whole procedure, trained beseeching eyes on Cole.

"Hey, girl," he breathed in wonder and wriggled over to where she lay. "You've been busy."

He laughed as one particularly fat puppy who'd been resting on top of his siblings rolled off the pack and over to where Cole was. "Hi, there, little fella," he said, stroking the soft fur and rubbing the chubby pink tummy. "Molly will flip when she sees you guys," he prophesied. Scooting closer to AWOL, he nudged the puppy back to the litter, moving the light as he went.

Cole smiled broadly. Looked like little mama here had made a nest, he noted, taking in the strange assortment of odds and ends that AWOL had collected to make her new family comfortable.

So that's what had happened to that new bath towel. Well, it wasn't new any more. He shook his head resignedly at the dog. And there were his socks, his underwear...

Cole shot a beleaguered look at the dog. She had stolen his favorite baseball cap, an old tennis shoe, his soft leather briefcase....

His backpack...and...an assortment of what looked like...test papers. Answer keys. Class files.

Oh, no.

AWOL. Not Lark. AWOL.

The burning realization that he'd made a tragic mistake suddenly began to dawn on him.

Buford's words echoed in Lark's mind as she tossed and turned in her bed.

Sometimes in this life, you have to get the old priorities straight. Put loved ones first. Pride second.

Should she swallow her pride and go to Cole? Somehow convince him that she hadn't cheated? But, then, why should she have to? He should know her better than that by now. She'd been sure their relationship was much stronger and more secure than that. In fact, she was almost beginning to believe that he felt as strongly for her as she was beginning to feel for him. Beginning to feel. Ha. She was head over heels in love with the big jerk.

But if he couldn't even trust her on something as simple as a silly test, then what did they have together?

Pride second.

She grimaced, realizing she was probably being overly concerned about her integrity. Buford was right. It shouldn't matter.

Sighing, she tried to disentangle herself from the sheets that had twisted unmercifully around her legs.

She supposed, if she looked at the whole thing from Cole's point of view, she would be suspicious of her test score, too.

Missing tests.

Missing answer keys.

No computer experience on her part.

And let's not forget she was the only person in class out of fifty-six students to ace the test. She grinned at that. It might come as a surprise to Cole that she'd scored perfectly, but he would have believed it if he had only known how many hours she'd stayed up late—after he'd gone to bed—and studied for that midterm. It was the only thing that had kept her sane, knowing that he was sleeping just across the hall....

The sound of a car door slamming drew Lark's eyes to the window. Could it be Cole? Glancing at the clock, she noticed it was just after midnight. She'd never known him to go anywhere at this time of night. Was someone breaking in? She wouldn't be surprised. Those little sports cars attracted thieves.

Peeling back the covers, she padded to the window and peered out into the darkness. There was definitely a shadow prowling around out there in the dim moonlight. It looked like someone was riffling through Cole's trunk.

Good heavens. She had to do something quick. She knew how much that little car meant to Cole. He would be livid if anyone so much as put a scratch on that brand-new finish. She should know.

Her heart picked up speed as she quickly pulled her jeans up over her hips and stuffed her nightie into the waistband. Jamming her feet into her slippers, she reached for the baseball bat that she kept by her bed. No time to call 911. She'd hide in the abundant overgrowth of her yard, and if she was lucky she'd knock the creep senseless. *Then* she would call the police.

Adrenaline flowed as she hurried down the stairs and snuck out the back door. Hearing the bushes rustle at the side of the house, she realized that the thug was making his way to the backyard. Afraid of being spotted, she ducked down low, behind some of Cole's shadowy furniture.

Ohmygosh. Ohmygosh. Her heart thrummed rapidly in her chest as she tightened her grip on the bat. She held her breath as he moved past, and suddenly she wished she'd swallowed her pride and gone to wake up Cole. He would know what to do.

As her eyes slowly adjusted to the lack of light, she tried to make out what had happened to the prowler. She could hear him, grunting and crawling around on the ground, and wondered just what the heck this idiot hoped to accomplish. All the good stuff was inside the house. And even that, if she was being honest, wasn't worth his time. Unless, of course, you counted Molly. She adjusted her grip more firmly on the bat.

No way, baby. She'd kill him before he laid a finger on one precious hair of her daughter's head.

Dropping to her hands and knees, she crawled to the edge of the porch and peered down into the yard. There he was! It looked like he had a flashlight, and if her eyes weren't deceiving her his legs were sticking out of the crawl space. Somebody ought to show this guy how to rob a house, she thought hysterically, nearly hyperventilating with fear. Well, if he was this stupid, he should be a piece of cake to knock out.

As she slithered along, trying not to let the bat clank against the stairs, she could see the legs in question begin to wriggle out from under the house.

Oh, no. She couldn't let him stand up. She would lose her advantage. Coming down the rest of the stairs, she stumbled and groped around in the darkness for the bat she'd managed to lose.

Where the heck was it? she wondered, panicking, as she realized that the criminal was already on his feet and making his way toward her.

Aha! Her fingers closed around the smooth wood of the bat, just as he passed by. Thank God! Stumbling to her feet, she let out a bloodcurdling scream and called at the top of her lungs for Cole.

"Cole!"

Judging the distance between herself and the criminal, she swung the bat with all her might and—spinning in several off-balance circles—ended up on her rear.

"Cole!" she gasped, as loudly as she could, considering she'd just knocked the air out of her lungs.

"What?" came the masculine reply from directly above her.

"Augghh!" Kicking her legs for all she was worth, she attempted to crawl away from this madman and into the undergrowth. Thank heaven they hadn't gotten around to landscaping. At least this way she had somewhere to hide.

"Lark?" Cole trained the flashlight's beam over to the noise that had just succeeded in scaring the stew out of him. He swung the beam around the heavily thicketed undergrowth and adjusted the puppy he held higher in his arms. AWOL, curious at all the commotion, had managed to extricate herself from her brood and trotted over to Cole's side.

"AWOL, where's Lark?" The dog thumped her tail happily and sat down at his feet. "Some retriever you turned out to be," Cole grumbled and called her name again.

"Lark, it's me. Cole."

Her heart thundering in her ears, Lark couldn't be sure if she was hearing correctly or not. The burglar was beginning to sound like Cole. She listened more closely. It *was* Cole. Embarrassed, she debated whether or not she should answer him.

"Cole?" she called tentatively.

"Lark, where are you?"

"Over here," she grunted, crawling out from under a bush.

"What the Sam Hill are you doing out here?" He sounded incredulous.

"I could ask you the same question," she shot back, feeling incredibly foolish.

Turning the light so she could see, he held up the fluff-ball that sucked enthusiastically on his finger. "I heard noises, so I came out to explore."

With much huffing and puffing she took his hand and pulled herself to a standing position. "Oh, look," she breathed, forgetting her fear, forgetting their fight. Taking the puppy out of his hands, she looked down at her dog. "AWOL had a baby."

"She had a bunch of babies. They're all under the house."

"Really?" She nuzzled the tiny ball of fur, and laughed when it took the tip of her nose into its mouth. She giggled. "Under the house, huh? Who would have thought?"

Cole rubbed at the knots in his shoulders, wanting so desperately to take Lark into his arms, to tell her what an idiot he'd been, to confess his love, to pledge his undying commitment. But he was afraid. What if she hated him now?

"Yeah. I sure wouldn't have," he admitted. "She has a lot more than just puppies under there."

"Oh?" Lark looked up curiously.

"Yeah." He had to convince her to listen, but he wasn't sure where to begin.

"Like what?"

"Why don't we go inside and I'll explain everything."

"Oh." She handed the puppy back to him. "No, thank you," she said stiffly and backed away from him toward her kitchen door. She'd nearly forgotten. He thought she was a thief. And a cheater. "I have to get going." She would just wait until morning and see for herself what the dog had been up to.

"Please?"

He looked so lost that Lark almost had to feel sorry for him. Suddenly, Buford's voice echoed in her head.

Pride second. Life is too short to squander on things that just don't matter none.

Lark rolled her eyes. The old coot had a point. Marching woodenly up her steps, she held open her back door and sent Cole a baleful look. "Well, come on. I haven't got all night."

Breathing a ragged sigh of relief, Cole clutched the puppy to his chest and followed her into the house.

Chapter Twelve

"Have a seat." Lark tried to sound confident and breezy as she gestured toward the living room. She didn't know why she was so nervous—she didn't have anything to feel guilty about. Holding her head proudly, she said, "I'll just put on a pot of coffee, so that we can ... talk."

The last thing on earth she wanted at this time of night was a cup of coffee, but she needed to get away from him for a moment or two to collect her thoughts.

"Sounds great," Cole agreed, and settled uneasily down on the edge of the sofa to play with the puppy.

Slipping into the kitchen, Lark wondered what Cole could have to say to her now, that he couldn't have said earlier that evening.

She grabbed a can of coffee from the cupboard and absently measured some grounds into a filter. He'd made his feelings perfectly clear, she fumed, as she filled the pot with water and dumped it into the coffee machine.

He thought she was a common thief. Not to mention a cheater. If he thought he was here to persuade her to turn herself in to the college equivalent of the principal's office, he had another think coming. She'd earned that perfect score. Her blood pressure began to rise.

Never in her life had anyone ever accused her of anything so underhanded, she huffed. Indignantly she grabbed the now empty pot and held it under the tap to fill it again.

Just as she was ready to march out into the living room and give Cole yet another piece of her mind, Buford's sage advice filtered its way in through her wrath. There were two sides to every story, she knew, as the water she was pouring into the coffee machine suddenly overflowed and soaked the front of her nightie and jeans, effectively cooling her blazing temper.

"Ohh," she moaned, grabbing a towel and throwing it over the soggy mess. Taking a deep, calming breath, she decided to stick with tea.

Buford was probably right. Maybe she should forget her false pride and hear Cole out. She filled the teakettle with water and pulled two clean mugs from the drain board. It was true, she reflected, thinking of her late husband—life was indeed too short. Okay, she huffed as she dug a box of tea out of her cabinet. She would give Cole a chance to explain himself.

But it had better be good, she mused, untangling the strings and popping the tea bags into the cups. She was sick of the men in her life not trusting her. Ben hadn't trusted her enough to confide in her about his cockamamy schemes or allow her to help him by doing their books. And now Cole thought she was incapable of getting a perfect score on her own. How insulting. What did she have to do to prove that she was a trustworthy adult? Go around wearing a Girl Scout uniform?

As she leaned back against the counter and waited for the water to boil, she had to admit that it wasn't so easy for her to trust any more, either. She'd been lied to during her marriage. Ben had more secrets and hidden agendas than a presidential candidate, and that was something she just couldn't tolerate. Never again would she allow herself to become involved with someone who would consider hiding something from her, no matter how seemingly unimportant.

Cole nervously shifted positions on the rock pile Lark referred to as her couch, careful not to disturb the sleeping puppy who lay curled in his lap.

"What's taking her so long?" he whispered to the pot-bellied tangle of legs and giant paws. AWOL's puppies had to be somewhere between two and three weeks old already, he mused, noting the lanky legs. No wonder AWOL was constantly adding on to her nest. Her brood was turning into a bunch of monsters.

Cole grimaced as the sounds of some pretty intense coffeemaking wafted toward him from the kitchen. He figured she was probably still pretty miffed with him, and he guessed he didn't blame her. It was all he could do to keep from running into the kitchen this second and beg her forgiveness on bended knee. While he was down there he could even pop the question....

No, he rotated his shoulders to relieve the stress that was building there, it was too soon. He wanted to clear the air about Sherry before he proposed. It was important to him to come into this commitment with a clean slate. No secrets. No hidden agendas.

The absurdity of the thoughts that were running through his mind almost had him laughing out loud. If anyone had told him a few months ago that he'd be proposing marriage—to his evil slumlord, no less—he'd have thought they were certifiable. But here he was, for the first time in his entire life deeply and forever in love.

Luckily, Lark was a wonderful woman. He had a feeling she would forgive him for his idiotic behavior over the test and she would easily understand his reservations in coming clean about Sherry and Jake before now.

He smiled down at the little fur ball in his lap. Yes, indeed, he was a lucky man.

The shrill whistle of the teakettle drew his eyes toward the kitchen. His stomach clenched nervously. Well, he hoped he was a lucky man, anyway.

Lark brought the tea service into the living room and set the tray down on the coffee table in front of Cole. She was careful to avoid eye contact as she strategically sat in the recliner across from him.

"I...was, uh...having some trouble with the coffeemaker," she stammered as she poured them each a cup of tea.

"Tea's fine," Cole said with false enthusiasm, and bringing the cup to his lips for a hearty swig, he proceeded to scald the taste buds from his tongue. "Umm," he murmured as the tears welled in his eyes. He was incapable of saying anything further.

"You said you had something to explain to me?" Lark queried, drinking her tea in dainty sips. He seemed a little emotional. Her stomach twisted with dread.

"Umm."

He could feel her waiting expectantly, as the pain in his mouth finally began to subside. As far as he could tell, his tongue was still there. He gave his lips a tentative lick. Okay, good.

Taking a deep breath, he began again. "Tonight, after I'd gone to...well, turned in, I heard AWOL under the floor."

"So that's where she's been disappearing," Lark commented, taking another polite sip of tea. So, he wanted to make small talk and pretend that nothing had happened. Fine. She could do that.

Cole nodded. "Yes. She's been building quite a little nest for her litter down there."

"Really," Lark responded blandly, wondering if he always accused his friends of heinous acts and then treated them as if nothing was wrong. This was an interesting side of his personality she was glad she was finding out about now.

"You can't believe what I found under there."

"Oh?"

"Yeah. She'd taken a bunch of my socks and underwear, a towel or two and even one of my baseball caps."

"How about that," Lark remarked. "I'll be happy to get you some new socks and towels," she supplied, hoping that this was what he wanted to hear.

"Oh, no. That's fine, really." The puppy in his lap stirred and yawned, and Cole stroked it gently with his fingers. "There were more important things than that down there."

"There were?" Great. This could get expensive.

"Uh-huh. I found stuff down there that I'd been searching for all semester."

Lark looked at him, still not comprehending.

"I found my soft leather briefcase, a bunch of missing files, my backpack..."

She could tell he was leading up to something important here.

"And...the file that held the test papers and answer keys for my C.S. 101 midterm. The midterm you aced. The midterm I accused you of cheating on."

"Oh."

"Lark..." he shifted toward her in his seat and gazed deeply into her eyes "...I can't begin to tell you how sorry I am."

"Oh."

"I jumped to the wrong conclusion for no good reason other than the fact that I have a number of events in my past that make it hard for me to trust people. Events that I wish I had told you about a long time ago."

"Oh?" Warning bells began ringing in Lark's brain.

Cole set his mug of tea down on the coffee table and carefully placed the sleeping puppy on the cushion beside him. Leaning forward, he looked earnestly into her eyes.

"Lark, I feel just terrible about the things I said to you today. I haven't ever been as miserable as I was this afternoon, thinking I'd lost you. I was such an incredible jerk and you have every right to hate me. But maybe when I explain about my past, you'll understand."

Lark waited, the dread gnawing at her fearful stomach, like a wild thing with a life of its own. It was as if suddenly she had been transported back to the lawyer's office, where she'd discovered Ben's other life. His secret past, which he hadn't had the common decency to clue her in on. And that news had had a devastating effect on her and Molly's financial standings. Cole's news would undoubtedly have no impact on her finances, but what about her fragile heart?

It looked as if she'd made the same stupid mistake all over again. She'd gone and given her heart to another man who was fond of keeping secrets. When would she ever learn?

Refocusing her eyes, she tried to concentrate on what Cole was saying.

"Before we were married... I should have known then," he said derisively, "but, love is blind, as they say." He shifted in his seat, warming to his subject. So far so good. She seemed to be hanging on his every word, compassion filling her eyes. This was good. Heartened, he plunged ahead, baring his emotional life, dredging up the past, opening up old wounds, all for the love of a woman. The woman who sat listening so intently as he poured his heart out.

"Everyone told us that we were too young. But I wouldn't listen. I guess I thought I had all the answers." He stood and began pacing around the room and felt Lark's gaze following him as he went, obviously enraptured by what he was revealing. Hell, if he'd known it could feel this good to confide in the woman he loved, he'd have done it the day they met.

"I thought she was perfect for me. Tall, blond, stunningly beautiful. I would be the brilliant computer professor, discovering new technology that would make us rich beyond our wildest dreams, and she would look wonderful on my arm." He paced over to the door and back to the area in front of the couch. He reached down and briefly stroked the sleeping puppy. "I had it all figured out."

Turning, Cole plunged his hands into his hair and raked his fingers through it. "Then Jake came along. He was unplanned, but I was thrilled. Even though it meant putting my dreams on the back burner." He paced around behind the couch, and past the front door again as he spoke, his words coming out in a passionate torrent. "But unfortunately Sherry wasn't content to wait for me to make it. She... took Jake one day and left."

Straightening his back, Cole paced over toward the door. He would never let Lark see how hard this admission was for him. Not if he could help it.

"When she remarried, her new husband wanted to adopt Jake. I was still just a kid myself... young and stupid. And..." his laugh was hard "...I let it happen. Looking back, I still can't believe it. It was the biggest mistake of my life."

When he reached the door, he turned to find Lark standing right behind him, as if she wanted to reach out and share his pain. His heart swelled with love for this selfless, understanding woman.

"I'm sorry, honey. I've been doing all the talking here." He looked down into her wide eyes and fell in love all over again. He was so relieved that he'd had the guts to finally come clean with all this business about Sherry and Jake. It hadn't been nearly as bad as he'd feared and he felt great.

Suddenly, he had a new lease on life. A future. A future grounded solidly in love. Unlike the sometimes fickle future of computer technology. Too bad he hadn't realized how important a loving relationship could be, until now. "Did you want to say something, honey?" he asked, anxious to get past his past and on with his proposal of marriage.

"Just this," she growled through her tightly clenched jaws as she reached around him and flung her front door wide open. "Get out."

Chapter Thirteen

Lark threw the door shut with a vehemence that knocked it, quite literally, for a loop. The old door casing, as yet unrepaired on her side of the building, was unable to stand the stress of her ire and finally—with a gasp of defeat—let go of its tenuous hold on the hinges.

Luckily, Cole was able to leap out of the way while the heavy old door hovered, as if stunned, and then fell with a resounding crash to the porch floor.

"And stay out," she yelled. Turning on her heel, she marched back into her kitchen where she sank down at the table, buried her head in her hands and cried.

Cole stood on the porch for a moment staring slack jawed at Lark's mangled front door, a thousand different thoughts traveling through his head, all with the speed of light.

A slow grin began to steal across his face. He could afford to be magnanimous, he decided charitably. He still felt great after his confession, even if Lark didn't see the beauty of it.

He was amazed at himself. Normally, he'd be shocked and hurt over her sudden dismissal. He'd gone over there, hat in hand, and bared his soul about his private past and the pain it had caused him, and she didn't even give a damn. And now, for some crazy reason, all he wanted to do was laugh.

Maybe, thanks to Lark, he'd finally learned a valuable lesson about not jumping to the wrong conclusion. There was obviously more to her anger than met the eye. And before the night was over, he aimed to find out just what that was.

The one thing he couldn't quite seem to understand was, why his having a son and ex-wife should bother Lark so much. After all, she'd been married before and had a child, and he didn't hold it against her. Quite the opposite. He couldn't imagine loving Molly any more if she were his own flesh and blood.

Cole's thoughts drifted to the child's mother. He couldn't think of a thing he didn't absolutely love about Lark. Her ambition, her willingness to try the unknown, her noisy, haphazard household and even her nutty temper. Stifling a burst of laughter, he took a step closer to inspect the damage. She also packed quite a wallop.

There was no way she could spend the night with her front door lying on the porch like this. It was an invitation to every criminal in Springfield. She might as well just put up a neon sign for the burglar.

He could feel his face scrunch up and his eyes begin to water, until he could hold it no longer. Unbridled belly laughter bubbled to the surface in wave after wave of soul-cleansing delight. Oh, man, it felt good to laugh, he thought as he sat down on the front-porch steps and held his stomach. For the first time in years, Cole felt completely carefree and unencumbered by the past.

* * *

The puppy Cole had brought in with him wobbled across the floor and flopped down across Lark's feet as she cried.

"Oh, hi, there," she sniffed, trying to focus on the little guy through her watery bloodshot eyes. "I forgot all about you." Reaching down, she picked up the bundle of fur and cuddled it in her arms. "You probably want to go back to your mama, don't you?"

The puppy nuzzled her neck and Lark felt herself dissolve into a puddle of tears all over again. What had she done? she wondered miserably. Had she just thrown away the most important thing that had ever happened to her? She'd never been so confused in her life. Not even when Ben had passed away and there had seemed to be no future for her and Molly had she been this distraught.

And as much as she was now sure that she was completely in love with Cole, how could she tolerate his lies? She needed complete truth and honesty in her relationships from now on. That was a pledge she'd made to herself at Ben's funeral, and it was a pledge she intended to keep.

But had Cole really lied? A tiny voice, deep in the back of her mind, argued his case. He hadn't been completely open and honest with her about his past, but he hadn't exactly lied, either.

Too much of an emotional wreck to think straight, Lark decided the best thing she could do for herself was go to bed and sort this mess out in the morning. Everything always looked much brighter after a good night's sleep.

Standing up with the puppy, she turned off the kitchen light and headed to the living room. She stopped at the lamp by the couch and twisting the knob sank the room into darkness. As she shuffled toward the stairs she felt the cool breeze reach her from the front door.

Or what used to be her front door, at any rate. Sighing, she stepped over to have a look at what she'd done...and screamed.

For there, standing on her front porch, was a man. And he was laughing like a hyena.

Cole caught her before she could fall all the way to the floor.

"Lark, honey," he gasped, as her fright only fueled his sense of the absurd. "It's just me," he informed her, biting down on the scalded flesh that had once been his tongue, in an effort to control his hysterics. "Cole."

She clutched the puppy with one hand and her pounding heart with the other as she stared up into his mirth-filled face. "What is so damn funny?" she asked, annoyed that he wasn't as miserable as she was.

Knowing he was in the doghouse, Cole hung his head. If he had any hope at all of winning her back, he'd have to play it cool.

"Nothing," he forced out through his tightly pursed lips. He pulled his lower lip between his teeth and clamped down to prevent it from twitching.

"Good," she snapped. Eyeing him suspiciously, she took a step back. She couldn't think straight with his hand on her shoulder like that. "What are you still doing out here?"

She was furious with him for not trusting her with his past and she wanted to keep it that way. She wasn't ready to laugh it off as some petty misunderstanding. Although she had to admit there was a certain amount of humor in the way she'd ordered him out and then thrown her front door after him. Her lips curved imperceptibly.

He glanced down at the door that lay on her porch floor and raked his hand over his mouth, where he hid his laughter with a few feeble coughs.

"I ah...thought we'd probably better see about getting your door back on its hinges...ha...umm, tonight, here. You and Molly can't stay all night in a place with...ah... hem..." he coughed again "...ah...no front door."

When she didn't respond, other than to stare strangely at him, he grew slightly defensive.

"Hey, it's either that or I sit out here all night and guard the place. I'm not wild about that idea, so I vote we go get my tool belt." He couldn't look at her. He still wanted to laugh.

"Yes, of course, you're right," she stammered, feeling incredibly foolish. Why was he being so nice to her? She'd just thrown him out.

"Okay, then." Stepping over the door, he brushed past her and strode over to the pile of tools and remodeling supplies they kept on the floor near the kitchen door. Sorting through the mess, he extracted his tool belt and strapped it on, checking to make sure it contained everything he would need to rehang the door. "Grab me the cordless drill, will you?" he ordered, brushing past her again on his way to the door.

Her traitorous body warmed in reaction to his touch. She wanted to stay angry, to make him suffer for his lack of trust. But he was making it hard. It was glaringly obvious that if she so much as smiled at him he would keel over in paroxysms of hilarity. Narrowing her eyes at the twitch in his lips, she attempted to reassert her grip on her ill humor.

She set the puppy down in the kitchen with a bowl of water and rummaged through Cole's now impressive pile of electrical tools. Shoving the drill into his hands, she stood back and watched as he screwed her doorframe back together and repositioned the hinges, fitting them with longer, heavier hardware.

"That oughta do it for now," he announced, still unable to look her directly in the eye. "Okay." He glanced down at the other end of the door and grinned into his arm as he supported his. "If you want to grab the other end, there and hold 'er steady, I'll lift it up and pop the pins back in the hinges."

Lark grudgingly obliged. She struggled with her end of the door—trying to hold it still while Cole lined up the hinges—muttering under her breath all the while. "Son of a gun, ouch... oh, for crying out loud... this is the most... criminy... damn."

Cole listened to her diatribe with barely concealed amusement. She was madder than a race-car driver at rush hour. "You all right?"

"Just shut up and hang the door."

"Okay." He really had ruined a perfect exit scene for her. No wonder she was so hot under the collar. She couldn't sulk properly with him there. Hiding a smile, he lined up the hinges and sank the pins. "Okay, you can let go now," he instructed and stood back only to have the immense, old door rip the screws out of the rotting door case and crash back down to the floor.

A cloud of dust rose, and when it cleared Lark could see that her door was no longer in one piece.

Cole hooted. "Wait a second, isn't this how we met?" he asked, nudging the pile of splinters with his toe. "Thank God my car is out at the curb. It is, isn't it?" He peered under what was left of the door, as if looking for a dented fender.

Lark, far and away beyond her ability to endure, couldn't take another minute. Unable to even speak, she choked on a sob and attempted to brush past him into the house.

"Lark, wait." Suddenly, Cole was serious, all traces of laughter gone from his face. Reaching out, he barricaded the door with his arm, forcing her to stop in front of him. "Please. We need to talk."

Talking was the last thing she wanted. An exasperated cry escaped her lips as she glanced impatiently around for a way to flee. There was none. She was stuck. Now she was going to have to stand here and listen to him defend his decision not to trust her. With his past. With his midterm.

"What?" she cried, anxious to get away from him and into the house where she could hide and lick her wounds. She'd borne enough humiliation for one day.

"I..." He tilted her chin until she had to look him in the eyes and leaned down to bridge the distance between their faces. "Just wanted to tell you that I love you."

When she simply stared at him, speechless, he continued. "I also wanted you to know how sorry I am that I didn't tell you about Sherry and my son before. I can see how wrong that was, in light of the fact that I have been in love with you for quite a while now." Dropping his hand from the doorframe, he leaned against the wall and smiled wearily. "I don't have any excuses, except to tell you that I'm afraid of being hurt again."

Lark was too overcome with emotion to formulate any kind of cohesive sentence.

"Please, honey." His voice was incredibly gentle and filled with understanding. "I couldn't stand it if you threw what we have away over a couple of stupid mistakes on my part."

In a complete fog, Lark left Cole standing in the doorway and wandered over to the porch steps where she sat down and sagged against the newel post. Her head was swirling with emotions and she wasn't sure whether she was going to laugh or cry.

Was this to be the story of her life? Ben had told her he loved her, too, and that hadn't stopped him from hiding

things from her. It hadn't stopped him from not completely trusting her enough to open up and share his whole
life.

On the other hand, Cole wasn't Ben.

In fact, there were very few similarities between the two
at all. Ben was a dreamer. Cole was a doer.

She could feel the warmth of his body as he lowered himself to the step beside her.

"What did he do to you?" His voice was soft. Understanding.

She shrugged, not sure she followed. "Who?"

"Ben."

Lark sighed. Maybe it was time to stop punishing other
people for Ben's frailties. Time to stop punishing herself. "It
was more what he didn't do."

"What didn't he do?"

"Trust me."

"Oh. That." Cole settled back against the top step and
studied her.

"He hid a great deal from me, thinking I couldn't handle
it."

"Sounds familiar." Cole's words were self-deprecating.

Her lips curved ruefully. "No, not really. There was a lot
more to it than that. He wasn't there for Molly, either."

Cole winced. The same could be said for him and his relationship with his son. None of this was boding well for his
case with Lark. He took a deep breath. "And so you're
afraid that if you get too close to me, I'll do the same things
he did."

She nodded slightly. "In a way, yes."

"I don't blame you."

Her eyes widened in surprise. "You don't?"

"No. I feel the same way, about you hurting me the way
Sherry did. I guess that's why I overreacted about the mid-

term the way I did. I vowed a long time ago that no woman would ever be able to cheat me again."

"I did the same thing. Except, you know, with Ben." She nodded quickly, a glimmer of hope beginning to burn in her heart. She knew exactly how he felt.

He shook his head and blew a sharp puff of air between his lips. "Aren't we a pair? So busy avoiding another disaster we end up right in the middle of one."

The glimmer began to fade. He was trying to let her down gently. To tell her that Sherry really had ruined him for any other relationship.

"And you know what?" he asked, nudging her with his shoulder.

"No." She smiled wanly. "What?"

"There's no place I'd rather be."

It took a moment for his words to digest. He wanted to be here? In the middle of a disaster? With her? For the first time since that morning, her heart began to soar. "Really?"

He nodded. "Really." Turning toward her, he lifted her legs across his lap. "Lark, if there's one thing you've helped me realize, it's that I have changed. I've changed and grown in the years since I lost Sherry and Jake. But that's nothing compared to the changes I've gone through since I met you." He tucked her feet under his arm. "I know you may have a hard time believing me, considering how I treated you today, but I'm not the same man that so easily let go of his woman. Or his child. I'm happy to say that I have an entirely different kind of pride now. And..." nudging her feet out of his lap, he took her hands in his "...if you think I'm going to give you or Molly up without a fight, you're sadly mistaken."

"Really?" she whispered softly, her eyes sparkling a deep iridescent violet in the pale moonlight.

"Really," he breathed, as his mouth closed over hers.

His kiss was soft as the summer rain, gentle, caressing, covering her with its warmth.

"Lark?" He nuzzled her neck.

"Hmm?"

"Will you marry me?"

"Me?" she asked hazily.

"You, Molly, the dog, the puppies . . . Mainly you."

Pulling back, she cupped his face with her hands, smoothing the worry lines at his brow with her thumbs. No, he wasn't Ben. He was Cole, a man to be judged for himself, the same way he was willing to judge her as Lark and not Sherry. Yes, he'd made mistakes as a father and learned from them and proven himself worthy with Molly. Far more than she could ever have said for her late husband.

Did she love this man enough to risk her heart and marry him? Without a doubt.

"Yes," she whispered. "We'll all marry you."

Wild with relief, Cole pulled her into his lap and kissed her as though tomorrow might never come.

Cuddling into the crook of his arm, she leaned her head against his chest and looked bemusedly at her front door. "Cole?"

"Hmm?" he hummed, twining his fingers into her midnight curls.

"What are we going to do about my front door?"

Resting his chin on the top of her head, he surveyed the wreckage and grinned. "I guess you and Molly will just have to use mine tonight. We can camp over at my place."

"Molly will love it."

"Umm-hum," he agreed. "And one of these days, I was thinking that we might want to tear the wall between our places back down."

She laughed and gazed up at him in pleased surprise. "What about your textbook?" she asked, concerned about distracting him from his work. "I think I finally understand just how important it will be to the computer industry."

Cole studied the sweet face that had come to mean everything to him and suddenly knew that it didn't matter if his software innovations were ever the runaway successes he'd dreamed of or not. He would eventually complete the textbook, and he was content with that. Now, he knew he had something far more valuable than any amount of wealth or fame.... He had the love of a good woman.

Bending low, he kissed the tip of her nose. "Honey, nothing will ever be as important to me as you and Molly are. As long as I have you I have the world."

"Not to mention this fabulous duplex," she teased.

"What more could a man want?" he murmured, and pushing her back on the porch floor sealed their long-term housing agreement with a kiss.

*   *   *   *   *

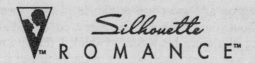

COMING NEXT MONTH

**#1096 THE WOMEN IN JOE SULLIVAN'S LIFE—
Marie Ferrarella**
Fabulous Fathers
Bachelor Joe Sullivan thought he had enough women in his life
when his three nieces came to live with him. But once he met
Maggie McGuire, he knew this pretty woman would make his
family complete.

#1097 BABY TALK—Julianna Morris
Bundles of Joy
Cassie Cavannaugh was ready to have a baby—and she'd found
the perfect father in sexy Jake O'Connor. Too bad Jake wanted
nothing to do with kids—and everything to do with Cassie!

#1098 COWBOY FOR HIRE—Dorsey Kelley
Wranglers and Lace
Cowboy Bent Murray didn't need anyone—especially not a sassy
young thing like Kate Monahan. And no matter how good Kate
felt in his arms, he would never let her into his heart....

#1099 IMITATION BRIDE—Christine Scott
When handsome Michael Damian asked Lacey Keegan to be
his pretend bride, Lacey could only say yes. Now she hoped her
make-believe groom would become her real-life husband.

#1100 SECOND CHANCE AT MARRIAGE—Pamela Dalton
The last thing Dina Paxton and Gabriel Randolph wanted was
marriage. But sharing a home made them feel very much like man
and wife. Now if they could just keep from falling in love....

#1101 AN IMPROBABLE WIFE—Sally Carleen
Straitlaced Carson Thayer didn't even *like* his new tenant, so
how could he be falling for her? What was it about Emily James
that made him want to do crazy things—like get married!

MILLION DOLLAR SWEEPSTAKES (III)

No purchase necessary. To enter, follow the directions published. Method of entry may vary. For eligibility, entries must be received no later than March 31, 1996. No liability is assumed for printing errors, lost, late or misdirected entries. Odds of winning are determined by the number of eligible entries distributed and received. Prizewinners will be determined no later than June 30, 1996.

Sweepstakes open to residents of the U.S. (except Puerto Rico), Canada, Europe and Taiwan who are 18 years of age or older. All applicable laws and regulations apply. Sweepstakes offer void wherever prohibited by law. Values of all prizes are in U.S. currency. This sweepstakes is presented by Torstar Corp., its subsidiaries and affiliates, in conjunction with book, merchandise and/or product offerings. For a copy of the Official Rules send a self-addressed, stamped envelope (WA residents need not affix return postage) to: MILLION DOLLAR SWEEPSTAKES (III) Rules, P.O. Box 4573, Blair, NE 68009, USA.

EXTRA BONUS PRIZE DRAWING

No purchase necessary. The Extra Bonus Prize will be awarded in a random drawing to be conducted no later than 5/30/96 from among all entries received. To qualify, entries must be received by 3/31/96 and comply with published directions. Drawing open to residents of the U.S. (except Puerto Rico), Canada, Europe and Taiwan who are 18 years of age or older. All applicable laws and regulations apply; offer void wherever prohibited by law. Odds of winning are dependent upon number of eligibile entries received. Prize is valued in U.S. currency. The offer is presented by Torstar Corp., its subsidiaries and affiliates in conjunction with book, merchandise and/or product offering. For a copy of the Official Rules governing this sweepstakes, send a self-addressed, stamped envelope (WA residents need not affix return postage) to: Extra Bonus Prize Drawing Rules, P.O. Box 4590, Blair, NE 68009, USA.

SWP-S795

He's Too Hot To Handle...but she can take a little heat.

SILHOUETTE Summer Sizzlers

This summer don't be left in the cold, join Silhouette for the hottest Summer Sizzlers collection. The perfect summer read, on the beach or while vacationing, Summer Sizzlers features sexy heroes who are "Too Hot To Handle." This collection of three new stories is written by bestselling authors Mary Lynn Baxter, Ann Major and Laura Parker.

Available this July wherever Silhouette books are sold.

SS95

As a Privileged Woman, you'll be entitled to all these Free Benefits. And Free Gifts, too.

To thank you for buying our books, we've designed an exclusive FREE program called *PAGES & PRIVILEGES*™. You can enroll with just one Proof of Purchase, and get the kind of luxuries that, until now, you could only read about.

BIG HOTEL DISCOUNTS

A privileged woman stays in the finest hotels. And so can you—at up to 60% off! Imagine standing in a hotel check-in line and watching as the guest in front of you pays $150 for the same room that's only costing you $60. Your *Pages & Privileges* discounts are good at Sheraton, Marriott, Best Western, Hyatt and thousands of other fine hotels all over the U.S., Canada and Europe.

FREE DISCOUNT TRAVEL SERVICE

A privileged woman is always jetting to romantic places. When you fly, just make one phone call for the lowest published airfare at time of booking—or double the difference back! PLUS— you'll get a $25 voucher to use the first time you book a flight AND 5% cash back on every ticket you buy thereafter through the travel service!

SR-PP3A

𝒢REE GIFTS!

A privileged woman is always getting wonderful gifts.
Luxuriate in rich fragrances that will stir your senses (and his). This gift-boxed assortment of fine perfumes includes three popular scents, each in a beautiful designer bottle. <u>Truly Lace</u>...This luxurious fragrance unveils your sensuous side. <u>L'Effleur</u>...discover the romance of the Victorian era with this soft floral. <u>Muguet des bois</u>...a single note floral of singular beauty.

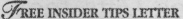

YOURS FREE!

$50 **VALUE**

𝒢REE INSIDER TIPS LETTER

A privileged woman is always informed. And you'll be, too, with our free letter full of fascinating information and sneak previews of upcoming books.

𝓜ORE GREAT GIFTS & BENEFITS TO COME

A privileged woman always has a lot to look forward to. And so will you. You get all these wonderful FREE gifts and benefits now with only one purchase...and there are no additional purchases required. However, each additional retail purchase of Harlequin and Silhouette books brings you a step closer to even more great FREE benefits like half-price movie tickets... and even more FREE gifts.

L'Effleur...This basketful of romance lets you discover L'Effleur from head to toe, heart to home.

Truly Lace... A basket spun with the sensuous luxuries of Truly Lace, including Dusting Powder in a reusable satin and lace covered box.

Complete the Enrollment Form in the front of this book and mail it with this Proof of Purchase.

PROOF OF PURCHASE

Offer expires October 31, 1996

SR-PP3